DA

FISH & BONES

FISH&BONES

BY RAY PRATHER

HarperCollins*Publishers*

This is a work of fiction, and all events and persons depicted in this book are fictitious. No reference to any person is intended or should be inferred.

Library of Congress Cataloging-in-Publication Data
Prather, Ray.
    Fish & Bones / by Ray Prather.
        p.   cm.
    Summary: Thirteen-year-old Bones, intent on collecting the reward for finding a bank robber, discovers some of the ugly secrets hidden in his small Florida town.
    ISBN 0-06-025121-2. — ISBN 0-06-025122-0 (lib. bdg.)
    [1. Afro-Americans—Fiction.   2. Race relations—Fiction.   3. Florida—Fiction.]
I. Title.   II. Title: Fish and Bones.
PZ7.P887Fi   1992   91-44227
[Fic]—dc20   CIP
                                                                        AC

For my wife, Myrtha

Contents

FISH & BONES

IMPORTANT: A Note to the Reader

From the very beginning I would like to clear up the
one big misunderstanding that may occur at the end of
this story: Although some of the people in this book
may appear to be real—a few may resemble someone
you know, or might've heard of, or could even have
once met—that is *just a coincidence*. This story is *not
true*. It was all made up by me. "Fish Baker" is just a
name I thought up, like all the rest. There is no tall
lady who did the things I say, even though a tall lady
resembling her could be actually living somewhere.
And although I know of a man whose body was never
found after he went over the falls, his name isn't the
one I used, and I do think he is really dead. Though
a town like the one in this story does exist in the
Northwestern tip of Florida, let me say this again so
there can be no confusion: It's just a story, like many
others you might have read, or heard someone tell.
And you can just ignore the dates, such as August
17th, 1971—they don't mean a thing. You have to give
dates whenever you write something down—and I
wrote this down twenty years ago—though it seems
just like yesterday.

"Bones"

(not my real name)

Summer of 1992

CHAPTER ONE

The trap set for me

FAR OFF IN THE DISTANCE near the city dump I saw a heat ghost. At first, it much appeared to be just a black dot hovering mysteriously in the hot air toward town. I watched it weave across Satan's Pasture and move slowly up the trail along the edge of our fallow field. The smudge wiggled in the heat ripples and grew larger as it floated on the heat wave toward me. When it got closer, I knew finally who was wearing the familiar red shirt, sparkling in the blistering sun, weaving up and down in his smooth, floating stride.

He wasn't whistling like he usually did.

All day I had made sure my exact whereabouts would be unknown, for there was a record heat wave the summer of 1971. It had been far too hot to do anything except what I was doing, until I looked across the field.

I swore and gave the branch above me a good whack to curse whoever had sent Fish Baker out so far in the hot sun to spoil my day. I quickly regretted I had banged against the limb, though. The jolt set the whole top of the tree bobbing, and my hammock jerked and dipped. The shock of seeing Fish Baker pop up suddenly across Satan's Pasture had made me forget I was dangling high up in a tree.

Fish carried doom about with him wherever he wandered. It wafted like an odor in hot air. I sense it every time I'm close around him. Sometimes I can even feel his sad presence from far off.

When he was six, Fish shot himself in the head by accident, with his father's old pistol. Two years later he got hit in the head by a fastball while he was clowning around behind home plate.

Fish had snuck into the ball game along with the rest of us. He shouldn't have been advertising his presence, but he boldly went out front on a dare that he wouldn't poke his head through the jagged hole in the chicken-wire backstop screen behind the catcher. The dare came from the shortest joker with the loudest mouth of Duck Tanner's bunch, a group of boys living—like me—in the black section of town, always trying to be tough, who were a few years older—maybe four or so—and bigger than we were. They had squeezed, pushed, and elbowed themselves into the crowd next to us, between the infield bleachers and the backstop, and were starting to bully us around.

Fish wasn't a reckless show-off. We knew he took dares so he could feel part of our group, to make up for his slowness. It didn't daunt him one bit to go and poke his head through the rip in the backstop screen.

I remember Fish did it almost eagerly, with a daredevil glint in his eyes. He smiled at risking his skinny brown neck so close to such razor-sharp wire, and he wiggled his scrawny backside at us. So we teased him back. I thought he was brave, but foolish; still, I cheered him on along with the rest of our crew, to show Duck Tanner and his bunch that we weren't chickens. But Fish chose the wrong moment to turn and lick his long red tongue back at us. He had put far too much faith in the butterfingered catcher.

Doc Holden was the pitcher on the mound that inning, and Doc was known for slinging meteorites that would buzz past any batter's ear. That frazzled hole busted in the chicken-wire backstop screen was evidence enough of his powerful arm. Doc might have made it all the way up to the major leagues except for what happened next in the bottom of the fifth. It gave him a nervous breakdown and he hasn't picked up a baseball since.

The batter didn't even see the pitch. Hoping to get lucky, the catcher had reached up blindly for the ball, but he'd only felt the wind go by. The umpire ducked just in time, as Doc's fast-breaking curve spitball hurled past at rocket speed, like a comet trailed by its own blur, appearing to pick up more momentum as it flew across home plate, high, but still in the strike zone.

It struck Fish Baker square in the temple.

A month went by before Fish woke up. He has never been quite the same. The real Fish Baker just went away and only a very little piece of him has ever come back. He was never a genius, but Fish can't even write his own name now.

The doctors at the hospital said repeatedly, "It's just an enormous shock to his system. Fish is a growing boy. He'll recover as time goes by. Most likely, he'll just snap out of it."

Five years have gone by and Fish hasn't snapped out of it yet. Our gang has broken up. I think we slowly drifted apart because nobody was willing to come right out and say who really issued the dare out of fear of a certain bad number of big Duck Tanner's bunch, who is really responsible, and of Long Mose Baker, Fish's older brother, who just might decide that the tipster was guilty.

I'm no rat who squeals. I am content to let it gnaw upon Short Billy's dirty conscience—if he has one— and to watch him sweat over the possibility that one day Mose Baker might find out the truth.

Duck Tanner and his bunch have all stuck around. Every last one of those dummies dropped out of school and now stacks lumber across town over at Cutter's Mill—something I sure don't plan to let happen to me. Long Mose Baker, mad at everybody because of Fish, left town three years ago to join the Marines and hasn't been back since. Fish is now Sun City's wandering whistler and mindless fetcher. He'll do anything he is told, without ever remembering he has done it, with a smile, and for free. But when his ma, Madame Baker the hairdresser, catches anyone using Fish as a gofer, she screams her head off and then asks for a decent payment, which she pockets herself immediately, since Fish doesn't know the first thing about money.

Some people say it would cause fewer problems if she had sent Fish straightaway to Chattahoochee, the state crazy house, five years ago, since she can't keep him locked up all day while she takes in her beauty-parlor customers. It's true—him running loose is asking for trouble. Too often, someone without a conscience who is bent on mischief uses Fish to do awful things, and will even get him to stop his telltale whistling long enough to hide the horrible deeds.

Although I sensed something bad was about to happen, a funny thought buzzed through me, and I had to smile. Even Fish Baker would never have dared trespass across Satan's Pasture so comfortable if my grandpa's pet bull had been still feeding there, but Satan was dead. He'd had to be slaughtered because of his bad behavior, and his terror is just a fading memory. But "Warning—Bull" signs still hang along the rusting fence. It's just a joke, now. Fish Baker can't read the signs anyhow, and he doesn't know what a joke is. I wouldn't do it, but if I were indecent enough to play a trick on Fish and say, "Fish, walk to the end of the world," I know he would just flash me an obedient smile and start walking. It gives me the jitters being around him, because I always have to watch what I say. Fish has got no mind to tell him certain things aren't possible, some things are just dumb and stupid, and many things you just never do. He will steal, too. Not for himself, though. Usually because someone else puts him up to it.

Now I was watching every step he took as he got nearer, waiting just long enough for him to get a little closer.

I grabbed the stout limb next to me, twisted out of my hammock, and started the long climb down to meet him. I wasn't about to let him reach my house before I went out to stop him. If any of my folks knew Fish was lurking around, they would get real upset. My mother alone would have a fit, since Fish has been known to snatch the latest fashions, especially brand-name ladies' garments, right off a clothesline.

I had a real strong feeling it was me he was after.

I'm used to the steep climb down the tree, but I was so anxious over Fish, my heart thumped against my ribs, and as I dropped from the last limb, my right foot landed atop the hard hull of a pecan that had fallen early. It was too green to crack, so the shell went into the hard dry dirt real stubbornly when I mashed upon it, and it felt sharp enough to come right up through my worn sneaker. The pain in my foot was so bad, I almost screamed. But as silently as I could I dashed quickly across the backyard, hopping along on one leg and breathing kind of hard. I tried not to make a sound. I didn't even cast a shadow until I ran out of the shade of the pecan tree near the stables.

I sprang quickly over the pasture fence. Nobody called out to me. I had escaped being seen. I went to cut Fish off on the trail.

He started his sad smile as soon as he saw me coming. It was so muggy, I was sweating like a soft rain even before I met up with him. Fish wasn't, not even a drop, and after his long walk from town in the blazing summer Florida sun. It has always amazed me how he manages to stay so cool.

The second I got to him, just as I began to sink into his forever-sad, flat, moist, dark eyes, Fish gave me a "Good day, Bones" like a windup toy. Then he thrust this note at me:

Hallo Bonapart!
For your eyes only, you understand! Meet me at once, at the city dump. It's URGENT!
J.W.C. (Toad Man)

P.S. After you've gotten the word, tear this note in a thousand pieces and toss it to the breeze. Your skin, plus mine, might depend upon it!

Toad Man has gotten me in hot water a bunch of times, and I knew his note spelled trouble. I tore it up quickly, but there was no breeze to blow it so I started scattering it along the trail. I was off right away to let

11

Toad Man know I wanted no part of his "urgency."

Fish never says good-bye. He just fades away silently and pops up elsewhere unless you give him something to keep him busy right away. I really only forgot him for a moment because the crazy note had me distracted. But Fish reckoned I had no time for him. He never even sticks around for a thank you. Just like a robot, he turned a half circle on the ball of his heels and headed back to town.

And he can walk!

I had to follow Fish to make sure he left our property. I started running to catch up to him. Beads of sweat began to run off me like a flood, yet Fish floated along, hardly leaving a track and making no sound at all. The ground was so dry, it had cracked. Next to the trail I could hear a hardy bird scratching around in the underbrush somewhere. Every last worm had to be far underground, for every blade of grass in sight was drooping in the heat. If I hadn't looked down in time, I would have stepped on a lizard's tail. Why is it traveling about in this heat? I wondered. Not one insect could be left to eat inside those dusty bushes. The lizard couldn't have been stupid enough, like me, to be trailing a poor soul like Fish, to go see an ignoramus like Toad Man, who was waiting comfortably up ahead in the shade near the city dump, while I burned my neck stumping across a hot weedy field. My nose was already ticklish before I got behind Fish and breathed his dust.

Since it was only half past five, the sun was still high

and had a ways to go before it set—in late July in Florida not until around nine. The air was so still, no leaf on any tree I saw was stirring. I could smell plums rotting on the ground. The closer we came to our orchard, the better whiff I got of the ones I saw still sparkling on the tree. I could practically taste their sweet juicy flavor on my tongue, and my mouth began to water. I wanted to stop Fish and eat a few, but my throat was too dry to holler.

Gasping, I trailed Fish to the garbage dump, where I saw Toad Man waiting for me next to a huge pile of fresh junk. Fish paused for more orders, like he was Toad Man's personal slave. Toad Man waved him on. Fish started up his whistle again and went off. Before an hour went by, some other trashy person would stop him for another dumb job.

I was real mad at Toad Man for what he'd done. It was bad enough that he had sent Fish to our place as his gofer although he isn't the only one in Sun City who uses Fish to do his walking—but Toad Man had the nerve to summon me and the gall to tell me to hurry, as if I worked for him. (It was him who worked for us—for my father, that is.) This wasn't the first time he had done it, either.

I was about to burn up, and I didn't bother to hide it. I was puffing heat as I started walking slowly over to the low dipping oak where he was sitting. I was hot, dusty, and sweating. There he was in the cool shade with his crooked back slumped in the curve of the tree trunk and his filthy rump perched on a scarred root that poked up out of the ground. The old chipped tree looked like it would uproot and rot away while he was sitting there. I began to wish it would, praying silently for a strong gust of wind to blow him and the tree away in a cloud of garbage, because Toad Man was far too relaxed, too comfortable there amidst those piles of scattered garbage to have anything good on his mind. In the middle of all that stench, putting on a look like a king getting ready to give orders to a servant, he gazed up at me with the eyes and mouth of a frog and a wicked smile scrawled on his scruffy, old, warty face.

I've always had a tough time figuring out just how old he really is. Toad Man won't say himself. If his yucky teeth were used to judge, he could be as old as the tree. He gives me the feeling he's been around forever, for he knows just about everybody's business.

I didn't like what I saw scratched on his wizened black face. It was surely a bad-news smile, a look I know too well. Toad Man gets a real pleasure out of teasing me by holding on awhile to whatever he is going to say anyway. He was waiting for me to draw him out.

"So!" I spoke first, to humor him.

"Well, good day, Bones!" Toad Man said, just like he had surely coached Fish to mouth it.

"I want no part of your chuckleheaded scheme, whatever it is!" I said to him.

"You don't even know anything about it yet," he replied.

14

"Still, I'm not the least bit interested."

"Oh, Bones!" he said, and laughed at me.

"How dare you send Fish Baker creeping silently around my house! You don't send for me in a hurry, like you're my boss! What've you gone and done now that's so rotten you've got to hide out here in the dump?" I demanded. Then giving it a second thought, I said, "Never mind, it's sure to be something I don't want to hear about," and started walking off.

"Now, that's no way to treat a dear old friend," he called back, chuckling. "You know we always been as thick as glue." I let him waste his time teasing my back while I slipped away. He is no dear friend of mine anyway, even if I did help him do something stupid once, in a weak moment.

"Thick as glue! Your memory is foggy, Toad Man," I shouted back to him over my shoulder. "And any personal problem you happen to have now has got nothing at all to do with me!"

"It sure does, too!" he said. I ignored him. His scratchy voice grew weaker the more space I put between us. "Of course, it is a bit of bad news," I heard him say, "but it's got possibilities!"

While he played cat and mouse, I faded farther up the trail, picking up speed as I went. Just when Toad Man saw I was about to disappear out of sight back across Satan's Pasture, he began to holler louder. "I guess you know where I just come from?"

I knew he had just come from work. I knew also he was setting a trap for me. So I kept walking. I was

15

pretending to be out of earshot until I heard what he said next. "Um sure you know what will happen tomorrow if I suddenly get sick and don't show up for work!"

Toad Man was using his nastiest threat of all.

I stopped dead in my tracks, like he knew I would.

My father is Sun City's garbage collector. He's got only one helper—Toad Man. When Toad Man is laid up sick, or just stays out for mischief, I get his job. In summer, it's unbearable.

This was blackmail, plain and simple.

I turned around real slow, squinting back at him. My blood began to boil. I shouted out as loud as I could, "What in the name of hell do you want from me now, Toad Man?" My message echoed back to me in ripples from far across Satan's Pasture.

Toad Man began to motion me back with a finger. I took my time walking back. He waited until I stopped just short of him before he said to me in a shouted whisper, "The bank's been robbed!"

I was sure he was putting me on. "Toad Man, it's too hot to joke around," I said, and he was also making me late for supper.

"Who's pranking?" he asked, with a smile too much at ease.

I took another step, and stood on both of his feet, on purpose, and bent down close enough to look into his warty face. I partly had to hold my breath so I wouldn't have to inhale his awful odor. His garbage smell came up to meet me. His yellow teeth—what's left of them— sure have never felt a toothbrush, I thought. I almost choked on the foul air seeping out of his mouth, curved into one of his wicked I-got-you-now grins.

I said, "You must be kidding me. Who in his right mind would ever think of robbing the Bank of Sun City? They hardly ever have more than fifteen cents in the safe!"

Too calmly, he replied, "Um not joking. The clever devil got a lot more than fifteen cents. Today the armored car from Central Bank over at the county seat made its usual delivery, like every Friday morning. Today is check-cashing day, as you well know. So the robber picked the perfect day and he made off with a real bundle."

If Toad Man was telling the truth, a seven-year portion of my weekly allowance I'd saved up was among the bundle. "This is not another one of your famous pranks, is it?" I asked, and paid closer attention to his rapidly darting eyes.

"Would I kid about losing my own money?" he asked. He sounded serious. "I got my account there too, you know. It's the only bank we got in Sun City. And that freckle-faced little talky teller, Betsy Gisendeiner, gave all our money away without even a struggle.

"Right after it happened, your father and I passed along to pick up the two barrels or so of garbage the bank piles up there every day. That window with bars on it, you know, the high one above the garbage cans? It's always open for some air to breeze through, 'specially in this weather." He fanned himself. "Sheriff Zeke talks loud even when he ain't upset. We heard

17

Betsy re-act the whole story over twice, for the reporter from *The Sun City Herald.*"

He appeared sincere. Still, I asked, while watching his face for some sign of a lie, "Did Betsy get a good look at who did it?"

"Much as she could with a gun stuck up her long nose," he replied.

"So?" I asked, and poked him.

"'Twas just one fellow, she said. All alone. At least that much she got out straight. Though the rest of what Betsy said seems to have wiggled out a little twisted, if you ask me. Because I heard the sheriff say to the reporter something like, 'The story Miss Gisendeiner told before she calmed down differs a whole lot from the one she acted out afterward!'"

"How?"

"Too long and exciting," Toad Man said, smiling, "'specially the parts where she went on whining, making like her very life was threatened. She overtalked a bit. Still, it all boils down to one man who wore a silly-looking Halloween mask to cover up his face. Depending on which version of Betsy's story you believe, he resembled one of those funny-looking pigs out of a comic strip come to life.

"And listen to this," Toad Man went on. "According to Betsy, over the crazy mask the robber had on a pair of extra-dark sunglasses to hide his eyes. You know, the kind blind folks use? Still she swore, cross her heart, that even behind dark shades, she could see the color of his eyes—and they was brown." He paused.

"Get the point?"

Pig mask? Brown eyes? I wasn't sure. I thought on what he had said a moment. "Is that all the sheriff has to go on?"

"Nope, there's a little more," Toad Man continued. "Miss Geez said the robber also wore a jacket and tie. You know, to make hisself look like any ordinary businessman coming in the bank on payday to make a quick withdrawal. Though she said he was very quick when he stretched across the counter to scoop up the loot, just for a fast flash, his arm got uncovered right down there at the wrist where the insides of his gloves split into a 'V.' And although Betsy got but a glance of his uncovered arm, and just for an instant, you understand, she swore she had no doubt on this particular point, even though, as she admitted to the sheriff, a crazy mask can fuzz up your concentration. Betsy stood on her words when she said, 'Couldn't have been a white man, but that's precisely what he was trying to make me believe by the way he behaved behind that mask.'" Toad Man paused again to hold on to the last bit awhile. "You get the drift yet?"

Toad Man had a way of talking that always drove me up the wall. I could never be sure if he was telling me everything. I sighed. "You mean the robber was a black man?"

"According to Betsy," Toad Man replied.

"She's probably lying."

"For what reason?"

"I can think of a good one and I'm sure you can

too," I said. "To cause trouble. You remember how Betsy became high school queen last year. Jo Ann Grandberry, the black girl who ran against her and lost, believed the ballot box was rigged. A lot of folks believed her. She was better-looking than Betsy."

"Yes, but what if she ain't lyin'?" Toad Man said.

I scratched my head a moment. And the more I thought about it, the more a smile began to crawl over my face too. It would serve Betsy right. "What has the sheriff done?" I asked.

"Not too much yet," Toad Man replied. "His last comment was 'It's a very complicated mess!' And on that I happen to agree.

"It all started out like a simple, ordinary bank robbery. But now, some yet-invisible person has added some strange hocus-pocus!"

"Magic?" I asked.

"No. Tricks!" Toad Man said, and he got up and started to walk slowly around the tree. "Oh, several people in town could be smart enough to pull this off. Probably one of them did. The thing that really appears strange is that whoever it was, he was also in several other places as well, you see, and all at the very same time."

"I don't follow you," I said. "Isn't there at least one suspect?"

"Three!" Toad Man replied, coming around the other side of the old tree. "All members of Duck Tanner's bunch."

"Any one of them been caught and locked up yet?"

20

"All!" he snapped back sharply. "Just a while ago."

"Hold on a minute, Toad Man!" I said. "I thought you just now told me it was surely only one fellow who did it." He was driving me crazy the way he kept giving me just bits and pieces.

"They got caught separately," he explained unclearly. He was doing it deliberately to sucker me. I was ready to strangle him.

"And are they all guilty?"

"It sure seemed that way at first!" he replied with a sigh. "All three suspects had a crisp new ten-dollar bill inside their pockets. And all three bills carried a serial number that matched up with ones from the bank holdup."

"So the case is solved already." I shrugged and started to walk away. "Big deal!"

"Not yet!" Toad Man said. "The sheriff let all three of 'em go!"

"Huh?"

"None of 'em did it," Toad Man said smugly. "Just imagine that!"

"That's just not possible."

"Just what I figure too," he said, "but facts say otherwise."

"They had some of the bank's money inside their pockets?"

"Yup," Toad Man snapped, "and not one of 'em can explain how it got to be there!"

"They've got to be guilty then," I insisted. "No other way!"

21

"Nope," he said. "It seems like they didn't do it, after all."

"Why?" I demanded. I had to pull everything out of him.

"Because all three was at work at the lumber mill when the bank got robbed."

I thought a second, and asked him, "And who vouched for them?"

"Their boss, Mr. Cutter!" Toad Man replied. "It seems he was with 'em."

"And him?" I asked.

"Bones, Mr. Cutter owns the mill *and* the Bank of Sun City. He's not likely to hold up his own bank, now is he?"

I thought it over for a long time. "Just who could do a thing like this, Toad Man?"

He chuckled like a fisherman with a nibble on his line, and said, "If I knew the answer to that question, I surely wouldn't be sitting here at the city dump asking for your help, now would I, Bones? I'd be collecting the reward. The bank is offering one, you know."

I sighed and straightened up, trying to sort it all out.

"Imagine, one thousand dollars!" he said, and I saw a wishful glint flash in his greedy eyes.

"I could do a lot of things with a thousand dollars," I said.

"Five hundred," Toad Man snapped. "Half's mine—partner!"

CHAPTER TWO

Toad Man's mouse I wasn't

JUST TO GET AWAY FROM Toad Man fast, I said, "Okay," sort of carelessly. On my way back home I began to think it over. I had planned to stop off to pick some plums to kill my thirst, but I was so preoccupied that I strolled past the orchard before I realized it. I always have to think twice about anything Toad Man says. Lots of foolish ideas are forever popping up in his mind, and I have learned not to go for his bright ideas too quickly. Just recently, I put my trust in him again (another last time!), and again it was I who ended up in trouble.

This April, not even three months ago, Toad Man asked me to deliver a letter for him, saying he was too shy to do it himself. It didn't occur to me to ask myself why he hadn't asked Fish Baker to deliver the letter.

Maybe Fish was already occupied with some other crazy errand. At the time I thought Toad Man was too cheap to buy a stamp. I didn't tell him so, but I should have. And this was probably also another terrible mistake of mine. Because if I hadn't felt sorry for him and had gone ahead and called him cheap, like I was thinking, we would have started arguing, and if we had, my feelings of pity for him, which he always uses against me in weak moments, would have evaporated in a blink and in the end I wouldn't have gone and done a thing my conscience was warning me against.

I went ahead and delivered his letter to Mrs. Baby Doll Long.

Mrs. Baby Doll was just recently widowed, this January. Her late husband died in his sleep during the night after their New Year's Eve party. Early that morning Mrs. Baby Doll woke up suddenly with a bad premonition. She reached over across the bed from her and found her husband ice cold. Mr. Long's ticker had finally given out. Doc Schultz had warned him for years about his weak heart, but Mr. Long kept right on with his hard drinking. Before every drink he took, Mr. Long would always say, "I'm quitting after this last one." Then he would laugh harder than anybody present.

He was well insured. He left his wife a lot of money, and Mrs. Baby Doll gave him an expensive funeral. She didn't keep it a secret that she had lots more money left over besides. She bought a big new Cadillac immediately, and in February she added a wing to her house. In March she started back sitting out on her porch again, in the swing, all her gray strands gone and so heavily caked up with rouge and red lipstick that where her chin and neck met, she was two very different shades of dark brown—and without her black dress.

Toad Man asked me to take her a letter in April.

He was at least honest with me about what was inside. He told me he had fallen in love with a beautiful lady and wanted her to know it. He said he didn't see any reason for him to hold back, so he was going to propose, boldly, from the start. "However," Toad Man said, his wizened black face seemingly younger now, his eyelids blinking as fast as a hummingbird flaps, looking shy and wringing his hands so roughly I thought he was going to twist his wrists right off his arms, "I'm afraid of being rejected because of my ugliness."

His earnestness stuck me straight in my heart, as he knew it would. I said, "Okay, I'll take it for you, Toad Man." I can imagine how bad he must feel sometimes, walking around with a face full of warts, looking like the bark of a pine tree.

As I trudged heavily up her walk, Mrs. Baby Doll was watching me come toward her from her porch swing. She was going back and forth in a slow rhythm. Smiling, she said, "Howdy, Bones, what have you got there?"

"A letter," I said.

"You're delivering mail now?"

"No," I replied. "This is private."

"Who's it from?" Mrs. Baby Doll asked me.

25

"You'll find that out when you open it," I replied, walking on rubber legs. I had a funny feeling. My last steps toward her I don't remember much. I don't even recall handing the letter to her neither. I got away from her house as fast as I could.

Toad Man still swears he didn't forget to sign the letter on purpose. But I have my doubts. Mrs. Baby Doll never believed for a minute the letter was from anybody but me since I was the one who delivered it. Instead of being insulted, she was flattered. She even wrote a long letter to my mother and told her so, saying, "I'm tempted by your son's sweet offer. However," she remarked, "he is a bit young to be so fresh. He is just a little premature, although he is growing fast in a cute direction." After she had signed, Mrs. Baby Doll Long put on a P.S. and wrote "No hard feelings," adding the word "smile" to that last part, in parentheses, after sketching a smile.

My mother warned me to steer clear of Mrs. Baby Doll after she saw her pinch my cheeks twice in town a couple of Saturdays later. I didn't like the pinches either, "But wha-a-t perfume!" I had said.

So today I wasn't running full out like I normally would to be the first one to bring home the big news. Instead, I hopped the pasture fence lazily and slowly walked across the backyard.

"Just where have you been hiding out all day, Bones?"

I was so distracted, I hadn't seen my mother waiting

26

for me at the edge of the yard. I saw at least a hundred undone jobs she had asked me to do written in her X-ray eyes, and I was late for supper.

"Satan's Pasture!" I answered with a start.

She looked at me like I was a criminal. Maybe she thought I'd been mowing Mrs. Baby Doll's lawn for large glasses of cold lemonade and the big tips she was getting famous for, like some other boys I knew. After a long, tense, silent moment, her nose going over me like she was sniffing for the smell of perfume, she finally said, "Supper's already on the table." I dodged around her and skipped up the back-door steps.

My father was already at the table. Though he was looking toward the kitchen, his large round shoulders rising high above his chair, his square, dark-brown face squinting like he does when he's very impatient, a sign he was hungry and ready to eat, he hardly noticed me—though I resemble him most—but as usual he had an arm around Ford, my younger brother, who sat cuddly next to him, grinning up at him like the Cheshire cat.

Ford is nine years old and he's my father's pet. He can produce tears instantly and knows how to fake one of his flash asthma attacks so good it looks like a real one. It gets him a lot of attention.

Grandma was brooding at her usual post in the corner by the window. She sat hunched, with her violet-tinted curls hidden under a gray wig, as always with her back to the deep freezer. Old Satan's picture and blue ribbons hang above the freezer, and Grandma can't stomach sitting at the table facing them. She will refuse to eat anything, especially meat, if she has to sit facing Old Satan.

Grandma eats very little as it is, because she always forgets to put in her teeth and usually can't remember where she saw them last. It's easy to tell when because she refuses to open her mouth, even to smile, and she picks around in her plate. Then too, she complains her gums are often sore. So gazing out the window through her thick bifocals while we eat is one of her favorite pastimes.

We just let her sort of do her own thing.

As I eased down to the table, my sister, Bird—who is twelve (born just a year after me, though she'd prefer it the other way around)—got to the table tardy too, the same time as I did. I waited for some kind of reaction, but my mother didn't comment. She sat down, still obviously hot with me, because she stared while holding a steaming dish of juicy butter beans, the final item. Then she said to my father, who was still tickling around with Ford, "Rufus, bless the table!"

My father has never been much of a talker. It's not because he's a silent thinker. I think he became close-mouthed from handling garbage all day for most of his life. It's real easy to clam up over a garbage can. So he usually saves up whatever he wants to say until he sits over his plate. Something about the table—maybe it's our company—seems to open him up. Before he started the grace, he said suddenly, "I guess you-all haven't heard the bank got held up today!"

"You're kidding, Rufus!" my mother said as we waited for grace.

"Nope, I ain't," my father answered. "They got all of it. Our little town's catching up. We're getting to be like some of them crime-riddled big cities up north, like New York and Chicago."

Grandma's eyes had wandered as usual out the window to follow a past memory, or perhaps a ghost that only she could see, but my father's shocking news drew her mind back inside.

"Don't think I'm going to live much longer," Grandma said suddenly and not to anyone in particular. "I'm no longer against the idea of dying early neither, with the world the way it's becoming these days." Then quickly, she switched subjects. "Who is going to reimburse us our money, Rufus?"

In times of panic my mother can always be counted upon to remain as cool and calm as a nurse. She remembers everything, in perfect order, down to the last little detail. As she pumped up her curls, which were drooping badly because of the extra heat made by the kitchen oven, she said to Grandma, gently, "The F.D.I.C. will, of course."

I pictured the hard-to-miss sticker emblazoned upon the plate-glass, burglarproof front door of the Bank of Sun City: F.D.I.C. INSURED UP TO $40,000.00 ON ALL DEPOSITS.

"You have nothing to worry about, Granny."

"Just who's this F.D.I.C.?" Grandma demanded.

"The government!" Bird replied through her pecky

29

nose, making a gesture with her hands at Grandma that looked to me like wings flapping. Bird's spike teeth sparkled behind her wide smile. She was real proud of her snappy reply.

Bird's snippiness brought up my bile, reminding me of how she cleverly uses her closeness to my mother to get away with murder. Times I know how Grandma must feel, all alone since Grandpa died, having to put up with such haughtiness, and in her own house.

"The crook took off with everything?" Grandma asked.

"Every last red cent!" my father replied, holding up a slip of paper. "See this? It's a city council check for all the garbage I collected this week. Just worthless paper! Young Clarence, the mayor's son, whispered as he wrote it out that I should wait till the situation clears up a bit before I try to cash it. I asked around some. Nobody's got much cash on hand. Tomorrow Toad Man won't get paid neither." A hint of a satisfied grin was on my father's face. I smiled myself.

"That probably means no shopping then!" Bird said.

"And my groceries and, er, other things . . . ?" my mother said.

"How can you go shopping with no money, Mom?" Ford asked. "But then . . . what will we do for eating?"

"No need to go shopping," my father said. "We got plenty of meat already. There's still enough of Papa's old prizewinner left over there in the freezer to last us a long while."

Grandma gasped suddenly, as if she had been hit by

a flash attack of shortness of the breath. My father slapped a hand over his mouth and looked at Mom. But it was too late to cover up his blunder. In a moment the mood around the table changed.

As I mentioned, Grandpa's prize bull, Satan, had had to be slaughtered. I'll remember that horrible year forever, because it was also the year my grandpa died.

Grandma adored the bull as much as my grandpa did. Still, Satan even gored Grandma once; and his sharp horns tore through her apron. She escaped unscratched, but she left a zigzag trail of the purple string bean hulls she had meant to feed to Satan scattered all over his pasture. (Purple string bean hulls were Satan's favorite snack. He just adored their sweet juice.) No invader was exempt: Satan charged everything that wandered into his private territory. If it moved, he went for it, whether it was red or not, or Grandma, or airplanes crossing overhead.

That's how the trouble started. A few of the featherbrains who came by to gawk at him got bold enough to test Satan's speed. The last egghead who jumped over the fence to shake his butt at Satan for a quick tease got caught and scrambled. So the Florida State Livestock Commission—coupled with a behind-the-scenes push by Zeke Oxblood, the sheriff, who once offered a huge sum to buy Satan, but my grandpa turned him down—ordered my grandpa to put old Satan to sleep.

Bad temper aside, Satan was a celebrated, prizewinning 4-H champion. When my grandpa was given a simple choice, steak or dog food, he argued back,

31

rightfully, "Satan didn't start it!"

The sheriff came by, gloating, to deliver the final verdict.

Grandpa got so mad that he himself charged the sheriff head-on. Even at his advanced age, Grandpa rocked fat Zeke out of his tracks.

Grandma still insists it was the sadness over the slaughter of his pet bull that was responsible for Grandpa's premature death. Then she cries.

Sadly now, Grandma craned back around to face the freezer. She gazed up at Satan's picture hanging just above it. Her eyes began to water as they paused upon the bull's blue ribbons. Slowly, Grandma traced a cross over her heart and nodded respectfully toward the freezer. Some remaining parts of Satan were still buried down in the lower quarters, hidden under the frozen vegetables.

Grandma digs out a chunk, sometimes, for special occasions. Usually, she does it in remembrance of my dead grandpa, but only she is allowed to decide when.

"Things aren't all that bad, Momma," my father said, trying to console Grandma. Her tears came anyway.

"Did the robber have to shoot anybody?" Ford asked excitedly, ignoring Grandma's weeping.

"No, Ford! But he had a loaded gun stuck up Betsy Gisendeiner's nose. And already three of Duck Tanner's bunch have been arrested. Though it seems they're all innocent." I paused to swallow. I didn't like the sound of the word "innocent" so near Duck Tanner's name.

"The sheriff's already let them go," I continued. "Mr. Cutter himself vouched for them. He's offering a thousand dollars to anyone with the right information—just imagine that, a thousand bucks!

"Though up to a little while ago nobody was caught yet. So the whole town is a mess. I mean, upside down.

"And they say, well at least Betsy Gisendeiner does—you know her and how she talks—that it was a black man who did it, wearing a funny-looking Halloween pig mask. Now, just how do you like that?"

"How you know so much about all this, Bones?" My father twisted his dark, stubbled chin around to me and asked, almost jealously, I thought, since he knew the story already but had let me get ahead of him after he got distracted by Grandma's crying.

"I bumped into Toad Man out in Satan's Pasture," I said, looking over the table at my mother, who was dabbing at her face and smearing sweat and makeup on her napkin. "He seems to know everything about the bank robbery. I guess he doesn't realize it also means he won't get paid tomorrow."

My mother didn't notice me watching her, and she didn't comment because her mind was elsewhere. "So," she wondered out loud, "I'll be shopping on credit tomorrow, I suppose." She smiled.

"Let's not overdo things!" my father said sternly. Then he added, before starting the grace, like it was a prayer he was saying aloud, "Let's hope this situation doesn't blow up. There's already enough that's sticky in this town between blacks and whites."

For a long while I had been gazing out of the window, like Grandma. Bird startled me. "Aren't you eating, Bones?" she asked.

I'd missed the grace too. I had been thinking about my father's comment. Like last year's high school queen incident, whether Betsy was telling the truth or not, the story could still cause some trouble.

CHAPTER THREE

My appointment with
Toad Man

S ATURDAY THE BANK WAS CLOSED. A note was
taped upon the front door saying PLEASE HAVE
PATIENCE. Because of the robbery nobody in town had
gotten paid on Friday, and now Saturday nobody could
even cash a check. The bank has always been open until noon on Saturdays, so a lot of folks got mad. A few
fights broke out. Every bit of trouble that happened
was connected in some way to the bank holdup. Very
little cash was floating around, so tempers flared up
easily.

The sheriff had his hands so full stopping fights, he
hardly had any time left to look for the bank robber.
One very disappointed man—who already had bad
credit—who was refused further credit to buy groceries at the Piggly Wiggly tore up his check, threw the

pieces in the manager's face, and then threatened to drive his truck into the store. There were enough people downtown trying to shop with empty pockets, waving useless checks and making promises, to cause long lines at cash registers in most of the stores.

Early in the morning, to dodge the rush, my mother had taken our truck—after my father had cleaned it up enough to remove all traces of garbage—and gone to town to do her shopping on credit. She stayed a little longer than usual. She also bought more than groceries—in fact, she shopped up a storm. Mother came back carrying a bunch of extra packages, as well as a just-out copy of *The Sun City Herald*. "Here, dear, read the latest!" she said, pointing the paper at my father. He was more interested in my mother's purchases. So I snatched the paper first.

Two items were prominent on the front page:

BANK ROBBERY BAFFLES LOCAL AUTHORITIES

Sun City has just a sheriff, Mr. Zeke Oxblood, and no deputy. Sheriff Oxblood prefers to work alone. Zeke has been the sheriff for as long as I can remember. My father says ever since he too was a boy. Up till now, not much trouble of this nature has ever occurred in Sun City. "Sneaky Zeke" often bragged that the town was safe and quiet because he was always patroling—being a white sheriff, he tries to ignore the racial tension that pops up from time to time. He himself started the rumor that he had many reliable informants, but it was a lie. Toad Man will snitch, of course. Usually, he does it for the extra money he often needs when he stays out sick for no good reason and sticks me with his nasty job. He'll snitch also to get even. Toad Man imagines people discriminate against him because of his warts. In his particular case, it's not only because of the warts or that he's black. I happen to know personally that his mischief helps.

Mostly, the sheriff collects an easy paycheck these days for doing pretty near nothing, except for giving out a lot of parking tickets. It's Sneaky Zeke's favorite brand of joke. He signs each one with a wild, curly zigzag to start "Zeke" and a wide looping oval to begin "Oxblood." He shapes the oval so it forms an egghead and etches a smile inside it to complete his autograph: a grinning ticket. He has even ticketed our garbage truck twice—both times by mistake. Toad Man and my father were parked next to a red-flagged meter only so they could go collect the garbage from the jailhouse cans behind the sheriff's own office.

Zeke is so eager to catch violators that he sits all day slouched down in his comfortable armchair, hanging slightly out of his office window, watching the slow ticks of the fifty or so parking meters along Main Street through a pair of high-powered binoculars. While he pans everything else in besides, he hunts constantly for a red flag that signals time's up, then he descends, like an overfed locust with a broad smile and a prewritten ticket. It's the fastest he ever moves. He likes late payers because there's an additional charge, which all becomes a part of his salary. "Bank Robbery Baffles Local Authorities," huh? I almost laughed until I saw the other conspicuous item:

LOCAL FOOTBALL HERO
PETER 'SKIP' GOODWEATHER TO WED FORMER
HIGH SCHOOL BEAUTY QUEEN AND
BANK OF SUN CITY TELLER BETSY GISENDEINER

Now Skip Goodweather is just five years older than me. Eighteen is awfully young to be getting married, I thought, unless something else was behind it. Skip fancies himself a playboy because he's got the words "Red Hot Lover" scribbled in curly letters on the fender of his fancy red convertible sports car. He flies all over town and disobeys all the traffic signs. He does it even in front of the sheriff, and gets away with it just because he's from a wealthy white family. In fact, Skip breaks all the rules. He's never with the same girl twice.

Betsy Gisendeiner, the bride-to-be, comes from the poorer white side of town next to the railroad tracks that border the poorer part of the black community—though as the bank teller with her fingers in so much money all day long, she puts on airs. I didn't remember ever seeing Skip with her.

Although Skip's family is wealthy, their Main Street restaurant has been losing customers lately. The Bar & Grill used to be the most popular place in town, though not if you asked anyone black. Not anymore even for whites, since Skip graduated from high school this past June.

See, he just did slide by, his grades were so bad. Some people even whisper that his father had to slip Principal Weatherspoon a few bucks so Skip could march. The gossip about a payoff could be all talk, since it takes a backseat to another very important fact: This past term, Skip's last, he ran up a new record on our football field, and it made the Sun City Rattlesnakes champs. He also clocked up the fastest hundred-yard dash ever run by a high schooler, giving him the fastest pair of legs in the whole state of Florida. That guaranteed Skip a choice pick of any college he wanted to go to.

During our Homecoming game, the last one of the season, all eyes were on him. The stadium was full. Everyone was expecting him to finish the season with a big bang. By his own choice, and because of the independence that went with the turf, Skip was playing wide wingback in an almost open field. He was running full throttle, wide open, chasing a first-down-and-goal forward pass with the four beefy linebackers of the Hunter City Bulldogs charging on his tail. Skip caught the pass, and the Sun City crowd roared, but the defending Bulldogs' linebackers caught Skip as he came down from his famous flying leap. They all hit the turf in a crunching bundle; the sound of Skip's kneecap snapping could be heard far up in the bleachers.

Since Skip's strong point had never been his grades,

instead of going on to college, he had to stay at home, managing his father's restaurant, the Bar & Grill, on Main Street. It's not exactly suffering. But Skip is not a bit happy about his turn of fortune. Ever since he was told by his family doctor he can never catch passes again, Skip's already hot temper got worse. Even though he mostly takes his frustration out on his fancy car, a lot of customers purposely stay away from the Bar & Grill now because of Skip's quick flare-ups when he gets reminded of sports.

He'll go up in a storm if someone just mentions the "football" word around him. Just last week a former fan, John Taller, asked Skip a touchy question as he was busy serving a burger deluxe to a customer. Skip never likes being interrupted. Taller shot his neck out of a booth as Skip went by. "Skip!" Taller called. "Reckon your leg'll ever heal good enough so's you can leap and fly again like you used to?" Taller had asked it innocently.

Skip got sour, and since action speaks louder than words, in a split second Skip executed a perfect kick to prove his point. His leg rose above the table and stopped just short of John Taller's nose. Skip snarled, "You see that, Taller? It's healed!" The kick was good, but it upset the burger deluxe Skip was serving. It flew over Taller's booth, skidded off one customer's shoulder and landed in another's lap. Two more angry customers rose and strode out the door while Skip's dad followed them, apologizing.

This touchy thing with Skip's leg has exaggerated

another bad situation that had been gradually improving, and made it worse. A rumor is whispered around town—and it didn't just start yesterday—that Skip's father, Mr. Pete Goodweather, was the secret Grand Wizard of the local Sun City branch of the national Ku Klux Klan, and that he was the one behind the cross burnings in 1965 when Sun City schools were ordered desegregated.

I've had a good look at Skip's father, Mr. Pete, close up. What's left of his carrot-red hair matches his red neck. He's got an ice-cold stare that's hard to figure out. His steely eyes slowly following me, him silently watching every move I made, the few times I've been inside the Bar & Grill, make me think it's all quite possible. I've asked my father about it a couple of times. He won't say yes or no. He looks a little uncomfortable, and says it's just best to forget about it and not to believe everything I hear. But that's no answer.

There's this other thing, though, that's not a rumor but a fact, and even now it still makes for a lot of hot and cold feelings toward the Goodweathers, especially Skip, for it was he without a doubt who sent Fish Baker into Abernathy's Swamp to bring back an alligator, alive.

Fish brought one back. Though it was just a baby, Fish had to have stitches up his arm like a railroad track afterward. Skip denies he sent Fish on the crazy errand. But it was to him, and nobody else—and to the Bar & Grill—that Fish delivered the 'gator. That's what points the finger at Skip, because on any errand,

41

no matter how foolish, Fish always ends up where he started.

Even without the Fish thing, which happened over three years ago now, or the rumor about the Klan, which comes and goes, there's something else: He's never gotten used to the idea I edged him out to win last year's champ's trophy, fair and square, at Sun City's Regional Rattlesnake Rodeo. Noosing the neck of the biggest rattler to take away "his" trophy was easy for me. I've always brought in the best specimens for the school's biology display, if Skip would care to remember.

For a fact, I actually spoke to Skip for the first time this year. Usually we walk right by one another without ever exchanging a word. We still don't really speak—we sort of just gibe one another if by chance we pass.

Looking at the wedding announcement now, I was thinking, I admit, how much I still envy Skip, the rich-boy side—though the marrying part didn't interest me in the least—when suddenly I heard a sigh in my right ear. "There's more to that there than's there in the paper! It should read, 'Poor Teller Marries Rich Playboy after Letting the Bank Get Robbed'!" Bird said behind me. She'd been reading over my shoulder, and had caught me off guard. Quickly, while I was still surprised, Bird forked her skinny fingers over my shoulder, and in a flash *The Sun City Herald* floated out of my grasp. She swooped off a step away from me, so I couldn't steal it back, and gloated.

Normally, I would rip her feathers out for such, and

Bird knew it. But I didn't argue. I had an appointment to meet up with Toad Man along the river behind his house. Ignoring her, I went silently across the kitchen to duck out the back door. I was in a hurry. Just off the backyard I cut down the trail leading round the back of the marsh, and in a few minutes I was standing beside our mooring on the swamp. I hopped inside my old leaky rowboat and shoved off.

Here, off our mooring on the flat water, so deep in the swamp, the river looks more like a pond and doesn't seem as if it's moving along at all—it drifts, just more slowly. It didn't take me long to pole my way through a water lane, which is too narrow to row through, duck under an overhang of branches, and squeeze through a thick reed bed to break out onto the river. Then I let myself drift slowly downriver with the current.

The river twists away from the swamp in sweeping curves. It actually goes right through the swamp. But inside that thicket it really can't be called a river anymore until you get far away on the other side. And I do mean far away, too, a long, long way from here, for the swamp is not little, by a long shot.

Our house is the farthest one upriver on this side of the swamp. We're sort of boxed in. Nobody I know of ever goes through to the other side of the swamp because of the many stories about what's out there. The stories tend to keep people away from the swamps. They are all made up, my father says. But I wonder sometimes.

Toad Man is our closest neighbor downriver, except

43

for the city dump. There is nothing else but marsh and reeds between our house and his. There is not much else beyond his house neither until the river bends to reach the Paradise Club on the edge of town. Then a little farther down the bank along the same curve, but hidden from the main road by a slippery clay cliff that's crowned with a crop of thick oaks and some stringy weeping willows, is the River Boat. Going past it on the river, with that giant paddle wheel that actually turns, makes you think it's really a riverboat that's run aground. Both the Paradise Club and the River Boat are just off the train tracks, for the tracks hug the river, right here, and both are further hemmed in by a triangle of vacant weedy lots. The triangle is known as the Bottom because it fills up with water and resembles a pond after a heavy rain. Nothing should be built here. Still, a few people (who get flooded-out every year) have stuck houses along the southern rim. Nonetheless, its broad sloping middle is so empty and bare, there is a clear view across the Bottom to the black Methodist church, which sits atop a lucky little rise overlooking all the Bottom and the rest of the black community beyond it. Just opposite the Paradise Club and the River Boat, though across the railroad tracks, which run through town separating the black community from the white one, is the football stadium and the school. The rest of Sun City curves—along with the river—out to Cutter's Lumber Mill, where it suddenly ends.

I could've walked where I was going, but it was hot,

and I didn't feel like dodging way around the city dump. It smells real loud when it heats up. I saw Toad Man standing along the bank near his house like he had promised me. Before I hailed him, I let the boat drift a little closer. Toad Man has no proper landing like most folks along the river. The bank along his backyard is a disorderly mess like the rest of his junky place. I waved to him and began to pole into the shallower water over to the side, seeking a good spot to bank. I settled for a bald patch I saw nearby and scrubbed up on the mud.

Toad Man had a disgruntled look on his old face, and I could see he wanted to hold on to his personal secret awhile. "Hop in before I slide back out," I said, "and remember, you'll have to bail out water. The leak springs up through the planks heavy whenever I take on two."

Silently he jumped in and shoved us back off in one move. Quickly I steered us out toward the middle, where the water is deeper and there are fewer rocks to watch out for. I rowed in silence and waited for him to open up, wishing he had taken a bath because I could smell he hadn't. He'd had plenty of time before I got there. All he'd done on this muggy Saturday morning was change clothes. Sniffing him was about as bad as the city dump I had just purposely avoided. The low-water rot in the marsh could never smell worse. I was glad the sun was coming down directly in his warty face. Unfortunately no wind was blowing. Even the honeysuckles I smelled wafting off the bank weren't enough to kill his awful odor. I wanted to ask him why he hadn't at least rinsed off.

Then suddenly he spoke, his old raspy voice still disgruntled. "All the clues I know about lead to a dead end," Toad Man said. "Two more innocent fellows got arrested early this morning because they had money on them that the sheriff traced back to the bank holdup. I hear Zeke grilled them real good. And listen to this: Not one could clear up how some of the holdup money got to end up in their pockets.

"Whoever robbed the bank must be planting it."

"Just who could be doing this?" I asked, and squeezed the oars.

Toad Man threw a hand up in the air and shrugged. "Could be that all of them're extra-good liars. Quite likely so. Or someone's trying real hard to put this thing on somebody else."

"Toad Man, do you really believe five people could all be carrying around money, money that they know nothing about, inside their own pockets?"

"Sure's hard for me to believe that, too," he agreed.

"And the sheriff?" I asked, steadying our course with one oar.

"Like the paper says." He shrugged. "He's baffled!"

"It has to be someone who wasn't working on Friday."

"I thought of that, too, but it looks like everyone in town able to rob a bank was working, or accounted for. All the usual troublemakers've got witnesses who can back them up, put them another place while the

46

bank was being held up. Strangely enough, that includes the ones who almost got locked up because some of the actual holdup money popped up in their pockets."

As usual, Toad Man had to tell me what I already knew.

"If someone is planting money, why didn't at least one person feel something while it was being planted?"

"No one seems to recall a thing."

"That's real odd!"

"The sheriff's a bit clumsy, if you ask me," Toad Man said, "but he did come up with one good clue. Could be important. Water spots show up on every bill he's got back so far. First person he caught yesterday, one of Duck Tanner's bunch, if you recall, surrendered a very wet bill to the sheriff. Second one, too, was a bit damp, I hear. Last three, well, all dry, but with those same suspicious water spots. Last person Zeke caught, just a while ago, thinks his wife must've ironed the bill dry, you know, not knowing it was in his pocket. Newest joke going around town now is someone's sneaking around, quietly stuffing money in other people's pockets while their pants hang outside drying on their clothesline. A clothesline plant is the only good, solid clue there's to go on, so far."

"The sheriff goes for that nonsense?"

"Bones, you ain't listening, sonny boy! Could they all make up the same story? Zeke gets tips. A-a-anonymous. By way of an unsigned note, or a quick-hang-up

47

call. It's this here little trick that points him to the right place. Talk is, everyone he's hauled in so far was truly surprised." His eyes studied me. "If my info's correct, there was no faking, just puzzlement over how he'd singled them out, and shock when the sheriff come storming in, ordering them to dig inside their own pockets. I can reckon for myself, they must've nearly got a seizure, too, fishing out money that wasn't supposed to be there."

"Who in town can pull such tricks?" I asked.

"Someone with fast fingers."

We talked about the lumber-mill crew, known for their ability with a deck of cards, but Toad Man said they were all accounted for, adding, "All of them not working was waving strikers' posters in front of the mill, making threats through the gate at the big boss when the bank got robbed."

"That's almost everybody I can think of," I said.

"'Cept for Fish Baker," Toad Man said.

"Don't be silly, Toad Man!" I said. "Fish Baker couldn't come up with a stunt like this!"

"Fish'll do about anything he's told how to do," Toad Man said.

"You're forgetting the unsigned notes sent to the sheriff. That rules Fish out completely. He can't even write his own name," I said.

"He can carry a note!" Toad Man snapped.

"Then you should know a suspect, too. Anybody can write a note."

"Yeah, that's true," Toad Man said in a lower voice.

48

"And anyone can carry a note," I continued.

"True," he repeated.

"Toad Man, will you please remember to bail out some water, too, before we sink!" I shouted. I looked around for the Campbell's soup can I keep to scoop out water. It was floating around his ankles.

"Sorry, Bones!" Toad Man snapped out of his semi-trance. "I had somethin' else on my mind." He swept up the tin can and absentmindedly started tossing water overboard. "Where was I? Oh, yeah, the sheriff's busier than I ever seen him."

After what I considered was a grand waste of time spent listening to Toad Man talk my ears off discussing what he called "strategy," just to kill time in order to give the Paradise Club time to fill up (in his opinion around noon), I was about to burn up. If I'd known just paddling around and talking was on his mind, I sure wouldn't have come to meet him so early. Giving him a look that he didn't even see, I said, "The key to it all is to find out who's writing the notes. How can we get our hands on one of those notes?"

"Clotheslines, notes—leave all that to the sheriff," Toad Man said. "Let's go where we're more likely to find a bank robber—in a saloon. The Paradise Club should be crowded by now. Saturdays, 'most everyone in town's usually there."

"Toad Man, we're not a couple of bounty-hunting cowboys! The Paradise Club is a bar, and, if you remember I'm a minor. I can't go in there!"

A sly smile appeared on Toad Man's face. "Don't

worry, Bones, I'll vouch for you," he said. "You're my cover, too, you see. I'm going to pretend I'm showing you the ropes. You know, sort of an older brother helping out, er, a younger brother."

Who'd Toad Man think he was fooling? This was nothing but a flimsy excuse for him to have a drink, though I had to admit I always wanted to see the insides of the Paradise Club.

"There's a good place for us to leave the boat," Toad Man said, pointing downriver at some high reeds.

I poled us over to the bank.

CHAPTER FOUR

My first time in the Paradise Club

PERCHED ALONG THE RIVER on the edge of town, at the very tip of the triangle known as the Bottom, are a few spots that my father always says "sprout trouble like weeds you don't have to water." Every last one was off limits to me. We stepped up to the door of the Paradise Club around noon. BE EIGHTEEN AND ABLE TO PROVE IT, the sign over the door read. My skin started to tingle. Butterflies flapped up and down my dry throat, but Toad Man popped open the door with a dangerous-looking thirst in his eyes. Cautiously, I stepped inside after him, leaving behind the bright afternoon sun. The slamming door scraped my heels. Inside the Paradise Club it was dark as night. I followed the sound of Toad Man's loud steps to the bar.

"What will you have, Bones?" he asked me as I bumped into his rear. My eyes were taking a little while to get accustomed to the sudden darkness, but I focused in time to see Toad Man wink and smile at the bartender, Big Richard, the owner, who was bathed in a halo of soft blue light oozing from a hidden spot somewhere behind his bar. Big Richard resembled a fat black ghost shaped like an overblown balloon. I held back a laugh. Behind him, a glowing mirror lit up an endless row of various brands of whiskey. The whiskey bottles reflected up a colorful spray of light, like a rainbow, the very first time I've ever seen one in the dark before. Through faint music drifting to my ears, I heard chubby Big Richard say, "The usual?" as his dimpled chin suddenly rose and his round teddy-bear nose twitched, like he smelled something.

To me, all the bar's smells mingled together over-powered Toad Man's singular rancid odor, but I guess Big Richard's nose was already used to those.

Toad Man acted like he hadn't noticed Big Richard's catching his scent. "The usual," Toad Man answered. "And what are you drinking, Bonapart?"

I hadn't realized I took so long to reply. "A Coke!" I snapped. "It's still early."

I saw both of them start a grin. I hadn't fooled any-body with my "still early" comment. Before the embar-rassment had time to sink in, some curious activity over in the dark corner to our right caught my eye. I saw a pair of familiar-looking heads duck suddenly down and out of sight. The two heads just appeared to vanish completely behind the high purple puffs of the fancy upholstered booth. Could Toad Man be right? Would we find some likely suspects hanging out here? By straining a little, I saw, though faintly, the man's shirt, which I couldn't put a name to immediately, and the lady's dress. I recognized the blood-red roses on a white background: It surely belonged to Skinny Mabel Jefferson. The only suspicious thing was that she obviously wasn't with her regular boyfriend, Duck Tanner; still, I knew one day she'd be bold enough to pinch my cheek in front of my dad and brag about having seen me in the Paradise Club.

My first impulse was to scatter, and I was puzzled when she suddenly ducked before I could. In a flash it occurred to me I had one on her like she had one on me. It made me curious. I didn't want to stare more than I had already, so I craned back around and took a slow swig of the fizzing Coke Big Richard had waiting for me. While I had been distracted, Toad Man had already started his own style of sly investigation.

"So few people in such a cool place on such a hot afternoon, Big Rich?" Toad Man asked the bartender.

"Almost everybody in town is broke," Big Rich replied, "except the bank robber, whoever and wherever he is now."

"Quite true," Toad Man said. "However, you didn't by any chance get any freshly rich customers in here today, now, did you?"

53

"Nope," Big Rich replied. "As you can see, my poor little place is almost empty. All the day long I've had just two customers, and you two, er, gentlemen make four." Big Rich cut a curious eye over at me, and a soft smile grew like he was happy to get our business despite Toad Man's awful smell.

I let my eyes wander slowly back over to Skinny Mabel's dark corner. "Er, you think we oughtta go over and have something to drink in a booth, Bones?" Toad Man said to me in a whisper.

"Booths are for couples," I said.

"We're a couple," he whispered to me again. "One 'n' one is two."

"Let's get out of here!" I upended my Coke.

"It's still early," Toad Man replied, mimicking me.

"But it's getting late!"

Toad Man turned his mug of beer up vertical toward the ceiling. He drained everything left in one quick gulp and set his glass back down upon the bar hard enough to crack it. Foaming at the mouth, he slipped his hand out of the mug handle, fluttered his fingers to limber them up some, licked his lips, made a delicious slurpy sound with his tongue, and burped. I was happy we were leaving.

"Let's go over and have one for the road in one o' those booths," Toad Man said and turned suddenly, catching me by surprise. It appeared to me that one drink was already more than he could handle. Even though I was curious, I grabbed him, and whispered,

"Toad Man, we can wait outside to see who the stranger with Mabel is."

"But we're already inside," he said, ignoring me, and with a drunk stagger, Toad Man began to weave across the dance floor toward the dark booths. He faded away quickly in the softly swimming specks of light that came reflecting off the spinning ball of mirrors, like the snowflakes on the card we received from a cousin up in New Jersey last Christmas. I followed him, but I wasn't amused because I didn't have the slightest idea what his next move might be.

All the booths along the dark wall were empty except the one Mabel shared with her guest. Toad Man had a wide choice to pick from, but before I could reach him, he chose the booth right next to Mabel's, and he took the best side.

I was a little mad. I slid into the seat across from him and crossed my fingers. Toad Man's form had nearly evaporated in the thick darkness. I squinted and saw he was pressing his crooked back against the divider and cocking his warty head high to listen. I raised up a bit myself. I couldn't see anything across the divider from over on my side, but I could hear low murmurs, and though it was faint, one whisper I was able to make out was "I love you." Surely one sound I heard was a kiss. Under our table, I pressed lightly on Toad Man's foot. *"Psssst!* What's the plan?"

"Sheeeee!" Toad Man shushed me and kicked my leg sharply. I had missed the faint form of Big Rich approaching with a tray. Quick and smooth, Big Rich set our fresh drinks down. He placed another mug of beer in front of Toad Man. I barely saw the Coke he put on my side. It was frosty cold. He had packed it with ice, the way I like them. I didn't feel a straw, but I didn't complain. Toad Man threw up a hand and waved a bill. "You can keep the change, Big Rich," he said generously.

"Thank you, sirs," Big Rich said, "and just holler if you need me again." I let him wobble back across the dance floor out of earshot before I whispered, "Just how do you know for sure how much money you gave him in all this darkness?"

"Simple," Toad Man whispered back to me. "I'm flat broke, almost, because I haven't been paid yet and surely you of all people should know why. I had just five bucks in my pocket when we came in here, all singles. I just peeled two leaves off the top and paid him. Single dollar bills I can count very well in the dark, Bones, thank you very much." Then he toasted me. "Down the hatch!"

"Cheers!" I said, as we touched glasses in the dark.

"To succes-s-ss," Toad Man said with a slur. He held his double s's. I squinted and saw him gesture a thumb back toward Mabel's booth with his mug tilted for a long swallow. My Coke fizzed a fine cool mist upon my nose as I sent it down in one gulp, too.

While I was still swallowing, an idea came to me that was so good I almost burst out laughing and sent the last drops of my Coke down the wrong pipe: I started to sing, and before I got even the first verse out, I let my voice grow gradually louder, and I started mispronouncing words as I went along, on purpose.

> *O lip to lip,*
> *'n' gum to gum,*
> *watch out stomach,*
> *hic, er . . . here it comes.*
> *O down the hatch,* hic,
> *'n' close the latch.*
> *Be sure ya swish it good 'n' round*
> *before you drown,* hic . . . *er, hee, hee . . .*

Then I paused, and burped loudly.

I slurred my way through several stanzas before I realized that Toad Man was kicking me. I gave him one back, and said, "Toad Man, I think he slipped me a beer instead of a Coke!"

"What?" I could hear panic in his voice.

"I'm getting tipsy, fast!" I said, louder.

"Huh?"

"I feel sooooo . . . dizzy!"

"Bones!" Toad Man's voice shot through the darkness like a bullet.

"OOOoooo . . . I believe um going to throw up," I moaned. "Oh, I see two spinning moons and a million fishes. How did I get so deep underwater so fast?"

I had a hard time holding in my snicker. It was a perfect way to drive Skinny Mabel and her guest out into better light so we could identify him. When Toad

Man finally figured out what my plan was, he tried to join in on my song, but he didn't know the words, so he quickly gave up and I stuttered on.

At first I got no reaction. Drunks do fall asleep, I thought. Merrily, I sung on alone anyway. In a few minutes, there was some movement on Mabel's side. It was my song that roused them, surely. But it was certainly the strong drinks they had been sipping that gave them the energy to climb out of their booth so rowdily.

Her partner came out first. Straight as an arrow, his tall silhouette bolted up suddenly in the dark. I got a little nervous when he looked my way. It appeared he was coming over to tell me to shut up. I began to fear I had awakened a sleeping beast, though the man seemed to look through me like I was glass. He didn't say anything—he just turned, suddenly, and ignored me. I thought they were preparing to leave until I saw him weave over to the jukebox. After he dropped a coin inside and made three selections, he looked my way again. He still didn't say a word. Mabel was sluggish climbing out of her side, so he wove back over to assist her. And slowly they staggered together, arm in arm, over to the center of the dance floor. They appeared to be swimming in the ocean of snowflakes the ball of mirrors sent waltzing around. Then they stopped directly under the slowly spinning ball, and he carefully steadied Mabel. When he saw she wouldn't fall, he backed off a half step and bowed like a star in the movies. Then he asked Mabel to dance. She accepted with a drunken smile. Slowly he raised up from his bow, pulled Mabel close to him, and kissed her. She hugged him back tightly, as if they were glued together. They stayed that way, stuck like icing on a cake, neither saying a word, while they waited for the music to begin.

I saw finally why I hadn't recognized the man's shirt. It wasn't a regular shirt but a military uniform. A Marines uniform, to be specific.

Long Mose Baker, Fish Baker's big brother, was back in town.

I knew just what to expect next. Underneath our table, Toad Man suddenly put heavy pressure on my foot and said, "Let's go. I just wasted two bucks all because a nasty little soldier is back home again!"

Long Mose sure can dance! I thought. Toad Man was already out of our booth and leaving. I slid out much slower than him, dodged around Long Mose and Skinny Mabel dancing, then followed him.

Abruptly, Toad Man pushed open the door. The bright sun nearly blinded me. He let the door slam back into me, but I caught it in time and dodged outside. I stepped on his toe before my vision cleared. I didn't bother to excuse myself.

"What's your big hurry?" I asked; then I smiled. I already knew his reason. He had gotten nervous when he recognized Long Mose Baker. Toad Man had recalled just how risky it was to go anywhere near Fish when Long Mose was around, let alone use him for a gofer, as Toad Man had done just yesterday.

I also knew exactly what was on Toad Man's mind. After Skip's alligator joke three years ago, Mose had strode into the Bar & Grill and had invited Skip outside. They fought all the way down Main Street. Neither one had let up for a moment even when the sheriff pulled out his pistol and fired into the air. Nobody could pull them apart until Mose finally decided he had beat Skip enough. And afterward the whole town nearly exploded in a race riot. Everybody just saw a black boy and a white boy try to kill one another, not a big brother mad because another boy had abused his little brother. "You don't like Mose Baker too much, do you, Toad Man?" I said as we got away from the Paradise Club in a hurry.

"Nobody likes Mose Baker too much," he replied over his shoulder to me, as I followed him along the dirty, graffiti-smeared side wall of the Paradise Club.

I had to walk real fast to keep up with his quick steps. "Mose acts the way he does because of the way people treat Fish," I said, stepping over some stones in the trail.

"It's not our fault Fish is the way he is." Toad Man twisted his head around and snapped at me, almost walking straight into the river because he was preoccupied.

I wanted to laugh at him, but he seemed so pitiful now. "That's no reason for people to abuse him," I said, but I didn't mention anyone by name. "It makes Mose mad, and he's right."

"Okay, okay, you got a point," Toad Man said, and

sighed, pausing to wipe some mud off his foot. "Maybe Fish belongs in a hospital."

"Institution," I said. "Fish is not crazy. He's just a bit slow."

"What's the difference?" Toad Man said, looking down at the river as if he was cursing it silently as we continued down the trail toward my boat.

"It's hard to say," I said. "However, for one real good example, you're crazy sometimes, with all the wild schemes you think up. Fish can't think, but he isn't crazy."

He turned his head around again and focused his frog eyes on me strongly. "But the point," Toad Man said, "is that Fish's wandering around loose is nothing but asking for trouble."

"It's Madame Baker who doesn't want to put him in an institution. She says she doesn't want Fish around the crazy people you find in those places. She says the silly nurses get them in slow and make them crazy with medication. And the government sort of turns a blind eye once they're admitted."

"Who explained all this to you so clearly?" Toad Man asked, his old raspy voice scratching in his throat.

"My grandma."

"She's senile," Toad Man said.

"But she isn't crazy," I said. He missed my point.

CHAPTER FIVE

Reverend Black's setup

T OAD MAN PURPOSELY HEARS just what he wants to. He had conveniently forgotten he'd black-mailed me into coming along with him in the first place. Now he was the one to get scared and run. Walking briskly behind him, I thought, He should be ashamed of himself, a grown man running away from Long Mose Baker, who's no more than twenty-one, if that. Though Toad Man's hair had been gray for as long as I could remember and I had no idea how ancient he really was, lifting heavy garbage cans all day with my father gave him quite a grip. I know. I've wrestled with him. So I wanted to laugh out loud. Instead I caught my breath because I saw Duck Tanner and his bunch—the thugs of the Bottom—coming down the trail toward us. In one big hurry they were heading to the Paradise Club, where we'd just left Mose Baker dancing with Mabel Jefferson, who once had been one of the nicest black girls in town, until she became Duck Tanner's girlfriend.

It was quite obvious they were real mad about something when they looked right through us as they passed. Not even Short Billy, the loudmouth of the group, said a word as they filed past. Fine by me. Toad Man and I got off the trail to let them go by. For just eighteen they looked like tired old black men. Finished. I knew Nat, Barny, and Jim had been arrested Friday evening for the bank holdup, and were let go for lack of evidence. That sure wasn't the problem on their minds now.

I hated every last one of them, still. Even after five long years, seeing them together always brought my mind back to our old gang—Darby, Lucky Strike, Fish Baker, and me—and that day at the ball game when Short Billy dared Fish to go out and get himself handicapped by Doc's fastball, while the rest of them pushed us around. I was thinking, maybe finally Short Billy is going to get his own brains knocked out now by Mose Baker. "Toad Man," I said softly, "we left too soon!"

After they were a safe distance behind us, Toad Man turned and squinted back at them. "No we didn't, neither. Now there's really going to be trouble!"

That ticked me off. What'd he think would have happened if we had run up against the bank robber? I asked.

"Call the sheriff," he answered. "Reward offer says specifically 'information leading to the capture.' It doesn't say a person has to catch 'im."

Typical twisted-thinking Toad Man! He'd really convinced himself we could catch the bank robber that easy. I had to get away from him, quick, before I got ruined again. I took a good look at how much water had leaked inside my boat, double-checked the knots I'd tied on both ends, and told him I was leaving my boat right where it was. On foot I could get away from him better.

As we left the river trail, a warm afternoon breeze was sweeping through the Bottom. We walked across the triangle of vacant weedy lots to take the shortcut to Orange Street, which runs through the heart of the black community. I'd looked all the way down the street both ways and had seen nothing, but suddenly from out of nowhere Skip Goodweather flew past us at high speed in his fancy red foreign-made convertible.

Skip had purposely veered over to the edge of the road so he could give us a bath of dust and gravel. His top was rolled down, so I saw he was laughing at us.

I swore at him. Toad Man cursed his family for generations.

Up ahead a bit, Skip slammed on his brakes and burned rubber until he zigzagged to a screeching halt. Throwing his fast roadster into reverse, he came back toward us, spinning his wheels madly. As he got back to where we were walking, Skip hit his brakes again

64

and slid once more. He was already famous for his skids. Most of the time, and from a distance, I thought it must be fun. But some of the gravel he had sprayed back hit me in my face. So I was mad.

Betsy Gisendeiner was riding with him, acting like she didn't see us. She held her ring finger up out of the convertible high enough to show off the diamond, to advertise their wedding on Sunday. There were no houses here in the middle of the Bottom. There was nobody around to see it, except us. This was not their side of town, although Skip liked to zip through the Bottom, I guess, because it was wide open and free. A lot of drivers used Orange Street as a drag strip—that is, up to the Methodist Church. Reverend Black always phoned the sheriff.

Skip drove around town so much with the convertible's top down, he was burned almost the color of his carrot-red hair, just like his father, Mr. Pete. Betsy was obviously scared of the sun. In the middle of summer she wore long sleeves. And she always had an umbrella nearby. She was white as milk, except for her freckles. She was probably afraid the sun would make them still darker, and then she'd be polka-dotted. Marrying Skip and driving around in his convertible would sure change all that.

"Guess the latest bit of big news," Skip called to us before starting to laugh. Betsy, too, was about to burst trying to hold down a giggle. I would've liked to punch Skip in his face, but Toad Man and I ignored them and continued walking. So Skip put his car into first gear and started to follow us slowly. I kept an eye on him.

"The sheriff's long list of suspects keeps right on growing." We still ignored him, so he added, "It's getting longer all the time." He chuckled before saying, "Y'all's Methodist pastor, Reverend Black, was just discovered with some money he can't account for!"

"Did you hear that, Toad Man?" I asked, in a low whisper.

"Uh-huh," Toad Man grunted back to me.

"It appears this money comes from the bank holdup, too," Skip continued. "Who knows? Maybe Reverend Black did it. Perhaps that's why the robber has been so difficult to catch 'til now. Who'd ever suspect a preacher?"

We just walked along and continued to ignore them.

"You ignoring me, Bones?"

I still didn't respond, so Skip shouted, "I know you hear me, Bonapart! Make sure you get this, too. I'm warning you now. Goes double for igging me. I'm going to beat you this year at the rodeo, you hear!"

I'd had enough of him. I shouted back, "You won't beat me this time neither unless a miracle happens. You been warned yourself now, too. You've got just two more weeks left to look for a miracle!"

"So, the walking dead comes alive," Skip said with a nonchalant laugh, and added, "I happen to know where to find a big rattler this year."

"You'll have to do a lot of searching to find one bigger than the one I've already found," I said.

Skip fixed a stare on me. I started to stare back. I

knew he was bugging me just to impress Betsy. Skip stuck his nose in the air and pressed the accelerator to make his engine roar. Betsy finally let her giggle slide out. She didn't have very much to giggle about, the way I saw it, after letting the bank get robbed. And she should've really been embarrassed by the exaggerated, self-serving story she'd told to *The Sun City Herald* reporter.

Skip floored his roadster and they sped off in a cloud of dust and gravel.

"There goes one real nasty fellow," Toad Man said out loud.

"That's just how Skip is," I said. "He still hasn't gotten over the fact I beat him last year. This year won't be any different, either," I added, "because I know a place where there's a rattler as big as a python!"

"Such a risky business is not worth the little hundred-dollar prize money you get," Toad Man said.

"By me, that's quite a bit of money for capturing alive the biggest snake," I said. And how dare he say such a thing, considering all the dumb foolish things he thinks up, I thought. Inside that nasty junky house he lives in, that he never sees fit to clean up, *ever*, among all his trashy belongings, there's probably even a snake sleeping somewhere, and quite comfortably at home, too.

"The Annual Rattlesnake Rodeo's still sponsored by the bank, ain't it now?" Toad Man asked.

"Yes."

"Well now, the bank's been robbed, if you recall, so

they've got no money left to sponsor anything 'til someone catches a bank robber, who might even turn out to be a preacher!" Toad Man said.

We were too near the church and the parsonage now for him to be talking so loud. "You don't really believe that nonsense Skip just now blabbed?" I said, ignoring the first part of what he said.

"Why don't we ask Reverend Black personally? There he sits now."

"Toad Man, up the walk! Not across the lawn!" I whispered loudly, too late to stop him. He walked by a DON'T WALK ON THE GRASS sign, right up to the porch where Reverend Black sat. How come he couldn't be as bold with Mrs. Baby Doll? I thought, pretending to clean a last bit of mud off my sneakers so I wouldn't have to look Reverend Black in the face.

"'Noon, Reverend!" Toad Man said, nodding his head and standing real boldly on the freshly cut lawn, which Fish Baker had most likely just mowed, free. Reverend Black didn't shout suddenly the way he normally did. So I looked up, slowly. Nearly popping out of his dark-brown face, the reverend's eyes bored into mine, probably making a mental note that I was with Toad Man while he was doing such a disrespectful thing.

Most of Reverend Black's short little body and porch rocker were hidden by *The Sun City Herald* but his egghead of pepper-gray hair appeared up over the paper. I saw right away he wasn't in a very good mood by the arc of his heavy, wrinkled hound-dog brows.

The newspaper was quite wrinkled too, but I saw it was the latest edition. It looked as if he had already read it through several times. After folding the paper, the reverend took a quick look down at his watch to check the time, and following a long silence, he replied dryly, "A pleasant noon to you both." Then his eyes probed us as if he thought we were the robbers.

"Certainly couldn't be true what I hear, Reverend?" Toad Man said.

"It surely is," Reverend Black replied. "Can't imagine who would put a thing like that on my clothesline, like a Halloween trick!"

"'S been the usual pattern," Toad Man said, pretending to be sympathetic.

"The sheriff seemed to know it was there before I did," the reverend added.

"'S been the usual pattern," Toad Man repeated.

"I'm at a loss for words," Reverend Black said, shaking his head. "After all, I'm a pastor! There's somethin' real evil at work here!"

I swallowed, and looking over at Toad Man, I said, "Sure is—and it's walking around on two legs."

Toad Man had missed my meaning. Reverend Black hadn't. Slowly his eyes wandered from me and fixed on Toad Man; then he said, again dryly, with his bug eyes magnified by his glasses, "It usually does, young fellow, oh yes it does, indeed. A pleasant afternoon to both of you," he added, cutting us off and ducking behind his paper.

Just like that he'd dismissed us. While I stood there

feeling stupid, waiting for Toad Man to get the message, Doris, the reverend's daughter, appeared suddenly at the screen door behind him. She had popped out of the darkness like a ghost and was silently waving to me she had something to tell me. We must meet later, Doris mimed to me.

I couldn't dodge Toad Man right away so I decided to play along with him until his money ran out. I suggested we stop for lunch in a place I knew he would surely have another couple of drinks, hoping that the beers would soon have their effect. But only toward late afternoon, after he paid twice and two other bartenders had picked up the tab so we would leave, did his old raspy, scratchy voice get the slow slur I had been waiting for. He said, "This here mad trail you're leadin' me down's gettin' quite wobbly!"

I had eased into the lead and was making weavy turns through the most crooked alleys on purpose, hoping to wind him. I smiled because he seemed to be quite drunk. My fast pace and the heat were doing the rest. Toad Man has to be flat broke, too, by now, I thought. How long could three bucks and the loose change he had last, even counting the freebies we had received? I saw my chance to get away from him until he added, "Well, Bones, let's call it a day. Um broke, and nobody's likely to give me credit."

He was still sober enough to reason, I saw. "I'm broke, too," I said fast, so he'd understand I had no money to lend him. He just shrugged. It was the honest truth, but he didn't go off and even try to beg a

70

loan, like I was hoping he would. Though he was right: Who'd lend him money? I had no choice but to row him home. And since my house was so near, and it was so close to suppertime, and since I'd already been late yesterday, making my mother quite hot, I decided it just wasn't worth the bother to go all the way back downriver in all that heat.

After supper, I lay up in my hammock recuperating from my long day with Toad Man. When I thought about how Doris had a habit of making her idle gossip seem so urgently important, I saw no reason to work up another sweat for probably nothing, when I knew where I was sure to find her on Sunday.

CHAPTER SIX

Skip's wedding day

DORIS WAS OBLIGED TO ATTEND Sunday School, and there was no way she could duck outside because Reverend Black himself was presiding. She couldn't get out of attending the midday services either, so seeing her before one P.M. was out. So on Sunday, a little past one, I stood at a distance watching the curious crowd of gawkers who had gathered upon the front lawn of the white community's First Baptist Church of Sun City on Main Street to see the year's biggest show-off. After wolfing down a cold chicken-and-potato-salad lunch, I left the rest of my family at the table eating in slow motion and complaining about the record heat wave. I had rowed stealthily by Toad Man's place and had come to town in my boat alone. Before he wakes from his noon nap, I'll surely already

72

be in town, I had thought. I was looking for Doris in the crowd when I saw the Bakers standing at the edge of the sidewalk behind me. Then suddenly, Toad Man tapped my arm.

He'd awakened and discovered I'd given him the slip. Before he could make a scene, I pointed the Bakers out to him. After he focused on them better, he remarked to me in a whisper, "That's surely a rare sight."

"It sure is," I whispered back. They were arm in arm like one big happy family. I didn't recall Mose Baker ever going out for a walk with Fish before he left town. He had always been ready to fight, and quickly, if anybody ever abused Fish, but mostly Long Mose Baker preferred to keep Fish hidden away at home. I wasn't sure why, but it seemed Fish's slowness embarrassed him. Now, while we were watching them, Mose Baker turned suddenly and caught us staring. He looked back at us with a bitter face. Madame Baker stared back, too, but blushing with pride in her two big sons, and of course the sparkling medals arranged in neat little rows across the breast of Mose's Marines uniform. Pulling them still closer to her with her two hefty arms, she squeezed herself still tighter between Fish and Mose.

Fish was apparently under orders to keep quiet, but he smiled sadly over at me. I smiled back. I didn't meddle him, nor go and jostle him, like I sometimes do. I sensed it wasn't the right moment. I could almost feel Mose Baker's penetrating stare burning my skin, searching for signs of amusement, first in Toad Man, then in me. It sure was odd, Mose Baker coming out to his biggest enemy's wedding. In that Marines uniform Mose Baker looked like an angry general ready to make war, rather than a wedding guest. He badly needed a friendlier face.

I snapped around abruptly and saw Doris. She was too far away for me to push a path to her through the thick crowd, and I didn't want to draw any more attention to myself by calling out to her. As it was, those nearby were reacting already, with their noses, turning around suddenly as they became aware of Toad Man's particularly strong flavor and noting that I was with him. So I suggested to Toad Man that we'd have a much better chance of picking up some possibly useful idle gossip, which might lead us to the bank robber, if we split up. That way we could cover both sides of the crowd standing on the lawn—separated by the church walk. Fortunately, he agreed it was a bright idea— though once he was gone, Doris still never turned around so I could wave, because she was too busy taking in the wedding gala and soaking up the gossip herself. And some of what I heard was satisfyingly vicious.

"Isn't this here a real storybook wedding!" Miss Striker, my last-term math teacher, said. The old lady didn't notice me standing behind her. She sounded jealous, touching her stringy blond hair.

"Certainly is," Miss Tooler, my last-term English dictator, said. "They didn't invite me either. I can't understand why. Just you looka there who's going inside!"

Her heavily lipsticked lips tightened, and as she stretched to get a better look, the saggy freckled flesh around her red neck unfolded.

"Dear Tooler, the Goodweathers didn't bother to invite anything but the cream," Miss Striker said. "We're not creamy enough, honey. We live too close to the railroad tracks." She looked around to see if anybody was listening to them, and lowered her voice some.

I pretended I was interested in the activity inside the church.

"Neither's that there. Look!" Miss Tooler said, much softer, pointing. "Margaret's nothing but a simple drama teacher, a substitute at that, and black, and she got invited. Why? I had Betsy twice for English. Twice," she added, "because she flunked out the first time."

"There's probably your reason right there, Tooler," Miss Striker said. "Betsy's real good at acting, the way I hear it, and inviting Margaret's an act! Betsy never did so well in my math classes, either, yet some-hooooow she managed to become a teller at the bank." She pushed up her glasses. "How awful strange life sometimes is!"

"Brains or not, she makes a pretty bride," Miss Tooler said.

"Well, I give her that much credit. But she can't count to ten."

"It doesn't really matter, if you marry a rich man, Striker," Miss Tooler said. "Being dumb's an advantage, actually. She can always come home from a shopping

75

spree and say, 'Oh, sugar, I forgot to look at the prices.' Skip'll naturally be understanding and not argue. God knows he's not marrying her for her brains, 'though Skip wouldn't want anybody to know his wife can't even count her fingers.

"And speaking of money, that reception they're giving afterward will probably cost them a fortune by the time it's over, because it's open to everybody. That general invitation in the paper, in big bold letters: 'Come one, come all, eat and drink all you can stuff inside at the luxurious air-conditioned Goodweather Bar & Grill Restaurant on Sun City's Main Street following the ceremony.' I'm quite sure everybody in town will be there, too, if you look around!"

"Huh!" Miss Striker grunted. "If you ask me, it's nothing but a thinly disguised way to beg back all the good customers they've lost lately because of Skip's bad manners!"

"I was just thinking—if we can manage to eat enough, it would be one good way to make them pay for slighting us. I can go through three portions myself. How about you, Striker?" Miss Tooler said, showing her buck teeth and elbowing Miss Striker with her fatty arm.

"That's just for the first go-round, Tooler," Miss Striker said, giggling. "To say nothing at all of more than one dessert," she added, wiping off some of her heavy sweat.

A laugh was pushing out of me. Before it did, someone bumped me from behind. I twisted around. I didn't see who it was. I did however notice that the Bakers, who had been standing right next to Skip and Betsy's wedding-getaway car, had suddenly vanished. The crowd had grown so big, it would have been impossible for them to run off without knocking someone down. The church lawn was full, the sidewalk crowd was spilling out onto Main Street, and a bunch of people still surrounded Skip's car, trying to get a close-up look at the decorations. A few people were even lazily milling about right in the middle of Main Street. The through traffic was doing a zigzag to dodge around them. How could the Bakers have just evaporated?

The church's clock was edging up toward two P.M.; the wedding was due to start any moment. I continued to look around for the Bakers, but my eyes always re turned to Skip's car, which resembled a laden rocket-ship with its streamers and tin cans attached to the back bumper. Pasted on the car door, inside a frame of real flowers, was a real fancy, gold-leaf, engraved and embossed wedding invitation with a full-color fairy-tale fadeaway of Skip and Betsy. It's what everyone stopped to marvel at before pushing deeper into the crowd.

The wedding ceremony inside the church was supposed to be private, but the church doors had to be flung open at the last minute when the air-conditioning failed. The midafternoon heat was sticky and damp, so all the windows got propped open, too. It gave all of us standing outside in the hot sun, sweating and gaping, a good view of the fancy affair inside. It was hard to miss the sheriff. Zeke Oxblood had conspicuously squeezed himself into the last pew beside the front door. Looking over his head, I could see all the way up to the altar. So I saw the minister giving Skip and Betsy the sacred vows. When the reverend said, finally, "I now pronounce you man and wife. You may kiss the bride," the sheriff got up to beat the rush. He ducked out ahead of the rice throwers, cleared himself a path and stationed himself at the curbside door of Skip's convertible. Then I saw him do a very curious thing. He looked quickly at the inside of Skip's car. His casual search was interrupted when Skip and Betsy suddenly emerged through the church's archway and trotted toward him.

The rice throwers began to shower them heavily. Betsy let out a feline scream of joy. A few of her jealous rivals were pounding her good. A row of cameras clicked. When a little boy on the lawn set loose a packet of firecrackers, the popping sound mixed merrily in with the ringing of the church bells. Everyone laughed and cheered about the firecrackers. Then someone else—who, I couldn't see—set off a cherry bomb. It exploded, sounding like a gun. The huge crowd parted near me, seeking cover, and almost stampeded. Some ladies poked fingers in their ears; others grabbed for their hats. Most men covered their heads with their jackets. Everybody ducked and shifted. When I realized it was just a cherry bomb, not a gun, and I saw the wide space that had suddenly opened up, I used the chance to get farther back out of the crowd.

It was getting rowdy and pushy. But I wasn't fast enough. I got caught between two waves of people, and somehow instead of moving away from the crowd, I got thrown closer to Skip's decorated car.

Bits of cherry-bomb shreds rained slowly down upon the crowd in a spooky silence that stretched to a full minute. When the smoke cleared, someone shouted a cheer and a chorus took it up. A sea of staring eyes followed Skip and Betsy along the walk. "A bright future and a house full of babies!" a heckler in the crowd shouted. Everyone enjoyed it. Then the snowstorm of rice started up again. So Skip and Betsy squinted and broke into a faster run at the middle of the walk.

I was scrunched up behind the sheriff, who was waiting for them at the car. "My congratulations!" the sheriff said when they arrived at the curb. His deep bass voice boomed over the other noise. He smiled courteously and opened the car door for them to escape. And, as the door popped open, a moment before Skip and Betsy climbed inside, I saw the sheriff's eyes fix on something on the floor. I stretched my neck to have a look.

On the floor mat lay a stack of bills over an inch thick. A white band, with the words "The Bank of Sun City" stamped in bold characters, was glued around it.

"How in the heck did that get there?" Skip shouted. Betsy's mouth was open, but no words came out. All three faces looked astonished. I couldn't believe my eyes. Betsy had herself claimed the robber was a black man.

79

A hush swept over the crowd. Everyone began to realize something was going awfully wrong. Like a locomotive, Skip's father, Mr. Pete, plowed me out of his way as he shoved through the crowd. He emerged behind Skip and Betsy, and his baritone voice broke the silence. "What in the heck is going on here?" he demanded, dripping sweat. His normally red face had turned much redder now, and the collar of his shirt was soaking wet.

Skip and Betsy were frozen like statues, arm locked into arm. Mr. Pete peered over Skip's shoulder and spied the stack of money nestled on the carpet. He craned around slowly, from Skip to Betsy, looking for signs of an explanation and saw nothing but empty faces.

"I am scandalized!" he shouted, and began to tear at his carrot-red hair where he wasn't bald already.

"I'm very much surprised!" Sheriff Zeke said. "I'm afraid I'll have to ask you both to accompany me." He never once took his eyes off the stack of money.

I heard Toad Man whisper into my ear, "There goes our reward!" How he had managed to get through the thick crowd back over to where I was standing I'll never know. Considering his smell, though, maybe they just moved out of his way and let him through.

Suddenly, on my opposite side, Doris whispered into my other ear, "Bones, I got to talk to you."

I completely ignored Toad Man. I half snapped around to Doris so I could keep my eyes on Skip and Betsy. I wondered how Doris had gotten to me through all the shoving people, too, until I remembered that Doris is real pushy herself. She cut her eyes over at Toad Man with a look that told me whatever she had to say, she wasn't about to mention it in front of him.

"Later," I said, with voices buzzing all around me. Every eye in Sun City was on Skip and Betsy as if they were Bonnie and Clyde. Solemnly, Skip walked around his car, looking like a dizzy, whipped, punch-drunk boxer who still hadn't accepted the fact that he had lost the fight. Betsy, in her long flowing white gown— the silk train that she had dragged behind her so daintily a moment ago soiled now, because a few eager people had trampled on it—was wringing wet, looking like a condemned queen walking to the chopping block. Neither put up a fight. They walked away quietly, almost haughty, staring dead ahead in space, not seeing anyone, it seemed, even Zeke, as they slowly followed him to his office, just a few steps down Main Street from the church.

All the way upriver, instead of doing as he was supposed to do—bail out the water spurting up through the leak in my boat—Toad Man did nothing but complain. "If we'd just looked once, we'd both be rich men now. We was standing right in front of it!"

I rowed us over to the edge of the river and poled until I scrubbed up on his muddy bank. I was kind of disappointed over losing the reward money, too. I really could have used a new boat. But I was glad to be rid of Toad Man.

As he stepped out upon the muddy bank, I said, "We just had tough luck." And quickly, I added, "I guess you'll be going to work tomorrow, then."

"Reckon so. There's not much else to do," Toad Man said, rubbing the warts on his cheek. Then he turned and walked up the bank.

He didn't know how happy he'd made me. I wasn't mad anymore about the flooded bottom of my boat. I wasn't even bothered he hadn't shoved me off. I pushed myself off with an oar and paddled out toward the middle, where it was deep enough to row calmly without watching for rocks. At the top of the bank, Toad Man turned and waved before he walked away. I waved back to him.

The mystery was solved. Now I could concentrate on other things.

Still, it was real strange to me—Skip Goodweather being a bank robber. He already had everything. I could imagine Betsy coming up with the idea, but not him. She had acted it out so well, and acting is something Betsy's always been good at. The rumor about Skip's father being a member of the Klan fitted well now, too. Why else would they have tried to pin the robbery on a black man, if not to cause trouble? It would be a perfect way to point the finger away from themselves. The Bakers had missed a good opportunity to see Skip humiliated in front of a large crowd, a well-deserved payback for all the things he'd done. What had Doris wanted to tell me that was so urgent she had elbowed her way through that rowdy crowd? With

Toad Man out of my hair now, I could go back down-river and find out. But if I rowed all the way back to town in this heat for nothing, I'd strangle Doris. I had to go home and tell everybody about Skip and Betsy first.

CHAPTER SEVEN

Rowing through Abernathy's Swamp

I F I HAD A MOTOR ON MY BOAT, getting up and down the river would be a lot easier. It's always been a tough fight stroking against the current. Even without Toad Man's dead weight I've always had to lean extra hard into the oars to get back upriver to Abernathy's Swamp. I needed to catch my breath, and before going home, I wanted some more time to think. So when I got nearer the triple overhang of branches that hides the outlet, I let my boat go twirling in the swifter current I met coming from the outlet. I don't know for how long, exactly, but I must have twirled for a while, because when I caught myself laughing at how strangely things had turned out, so loud that my echo was coming back to me sounding like a thousand different voices, I looked around me suddenly and saw

84

it was getting late.

I didn't waste any more time. I slipped my boat through the stand of reeds, being careful to stay far clear of the suck-mud bog. The outlet is right next to the bog, but it's almost invisible. I know what to look for.

Hardly anyone else ever comes this far upriver. The beginning of Abernathy's Swamp is the end of the line for most people. One or two adventurous fishermen might come as far as the suck-mud bog, but no farther. I use the boot graveyard as my marker. (Few who wade out as far as the reeds ever come back wearing both boots.) Nobody creeps any nearer the overhang. No one attempts to go through the outlet, even when someone gets lucky and stumbles upon it by chance. Not a single person dares go inside and around behind the blind into the closed-in clearing, yet it's so near, and always swarming with fish.

Every time I slip through the well-hidden outlet, I take a good look down at all the fish. All I ever see is fish, but the Abernathy legend still hangs thick in the air. The last known of the Abernathys drowned in the swamp almost thirty years ago, and the bodies have never been found. Most people believe the corpses drifted with the current slowly through the swamp and got lodged here at the outlet, unable to reach the river. If they are stuck here, somewhere down in the reeds or under the elephant-ear lily pads, their skeletons have never turned up.

Young Sheriff Zeke surprised the Abernathys on a

tip and caught them poaching alligators in a flat-bottom fan boat overflowing with hides. The hides were nothing but a cover for their moonshining activities. He asked them to surrender. They refused. Zeke fired two warning shots to show he meant business. It had absolutely no effect upon them. The sheriff's third shot put a hole in their boat. And while the two revenue agents with Zeke watched, it sank with the Abernathys inside. The slick Abernathys really could have held their breaths, swum underwater, and escaped. "Drowned men don't send up air bubbles," one of the revenue agents who saw bubbles claims. The bubble story has worn a little thin over the years, but still the Abernathy question is one of the reasons most people stay away from the swamp.

I was in a hurry. I looked quickly as I lifted the overhang, pointed my boat dead ahead, and eased slowly under the long thick leafy branches. It was very hot, and it was quiet until I spooked a swallow hunting insects in the shadows as I poled slowly by with one oar. Quick as I could, I skirted the batch of giant lily pads—they always slow me down no matter what I do—and I skimmed over the fresh crop of reeds growing up from the bottom. They scratched my boat underneath. It felt like a tickle. I was glad to meet the dim orange light of the setting sun at the edge of the long dark shadow cast by the overhang.

I poked the bow out into the Toe clearing, a name my dead grandpa gave it because in general the rambling swamp sort of took on the shape of a human body sprawled flat out. I pulled my poling oar up off the bottom, set it inside its struts on the keel, and gave both oars a roll. Slowly, I started to move across the clearing. Black water sparkled at me out in the middle, where the setting sun hit the ripples running toward the bank. Like a mirror on fire, a million sparkles flashed and danced on the surface. The clearing, which resembles a pond, looks small, but its appearance is very misleading. The elephant-ear lily pads cover up most of the water. I always imagine I can just walk across the whole swamp on a bridge of lily pads. But lily pads will hardly support a frog, while they hide many things underneath.

When I had almost reached the middle of the clearing, I looked back. The thick ring of cypress trees around the clearing, shooting almost up to the sky, made it look like I was hemmed in, and I would have been if it hadn't been for a narrow water passage. There is no other way to get through the wall of trees. I wasn't far from the water lane I was aiming for. I know all the passages by heart. I have to. No maps exist of Abernathy's Swamp.

Almost on the far side I split a huge lily pad I didn't see in half, and sent a bullfrog scampering to a dive. So smooth, he disappeared into the black water without a ripple. I eased up on the oars because I was near the lane, and I pointed my bow straight for the passage. Slowly, I sailed under the double overhang and into the narrow passage. The low branch rises up to about ten feet now. It was much lower to the water when my grandpa first showed it to me as he was teaching me the lanes.

Before I got too far inside, I pulled in my oars. There is no room for rowing inside a passage. I poled off the bottom. In a tight spot, I pushed off against a tree trunk to move myself along. I left the mouth, and slowly I merged with the darkness. I let the boat float awhile to give my eyes time to adjust. (I never use my headlight unless I get in a jam.) In the daytime a faint haze of light filters through from high up overhead. It's usually enough to see by in a squint. I can always distinguish clear enough between a tree and water. I see when to dodge. Nothing floating on the surface has ever surprised me before I saw it first.

As I wove slowly through the hazy darkness of the water lane, I started thinking. What if that money was planted on Skip, too? What if Betsy hadn't been lying at all? Pretty much all the others had been set up in a similar way, and later Zeke had had to let them go. Though the thing that really made Skip look more guilty than the rest was that all the others had been caught with only a single bill, and Skip was discovered with a stack. It was common knowledge that the Bar & Grill had lost a lot of customers lately. It could be that they'd gone broke, and that's a good enough motive, I thought.

In a few minutes I was pushing out of the lane and into the open Knee clearing. I let myself get a half a boat length from the last tree trunk before I reset the oars. And quickly I started rowing toward the old rotting landing along the Knee bank where I moor my boat.

My house is the last one upriver. I use the tie-up at the Knee because it's easier than having to walk way around the marsh to get to the river. Near the edge I fluttered my oars in the water to brake me and eased against the rotten mooring. The old wood gave and started singing. It hasn't ever been repaired—not even one board has been touched—since my grandpa built it some sixty years ago.

I pulled in the oars and set them on the floor, and hopped out quickly to tie up. Under my weight the rotting ramp boards bounced, sagged, and nearly touched the water. The old mooring posts began to wobble as I walked up the plank. I made a quick mental note, again, to bring some new lumber down, then I jumped off the end plank in a hurry to get up out of Abernathy's Swamp before darkness fell. The high trees block out so much light that it can look like night long before the sun sets.

The mud sucked at my shoes when I landed, and I nearly lost a shoe. I jerked my foot out and walked lighter until I got over to the spongy grass. After a few long, light steps, I left the clearing and cut into the trail. I didn't stop to scrape off my shoes. I wove quickly along the path, beating back bushes and briars with my pants legs. The trail rises in breaks. It curves and twists like a snake until it reaches my house. In two minutes flat I was at my back door.

I must have told the story of Skip and Betsy's arrest a hundred times before my family had enough. Each time, at the end, Bird interrupted me, saying, "I said yesterday when I read about it in the paper that there was something suspicious about that hasty marriage."

I reminded her that she had snatched the paper from *me*. And afterward, every time, Grandma asked the same question: "Where is the rest of the money?"

"The Bar & Grill is in financial trouble," I responded to her each time. Still, I fell asleep thinking about Grandma's question.

CHAPTER EIGHT

Monday-morning surprise at the Toe clearing

THE NEXT MORNING I wanted to dodge everybody, so before anyone was awake, I was dressed and gone. The sun was rising up over the trees as I walked into the Knee clearing; the pond was sparkling bright again. It was a good day for boating the lanes.

From far off on the trail I could already see my boat bobbing up and down on the ripples. I left the trail, bounced quickly over the spongy grass, and light-stepped across the mud to the mooring. Halfway down the landing, a plank broke when I put my weight on it. The next one kissed the water. I thought of the new lumber again. I also wanted to find out what Doris had to say, which seemed urgent to her, but what with fooling around with Toad Man I had already lost two good days of rattlesnake hunting. Although with

91

Skip Goodweather out of my way, I did have one less tough competitor to be concerned about now.

Before I climb into my boat, I always peep inside first. I once stepped without looking and surprised a spirity water moccasin sunning on the floor. I nearly sprouted wings as it sprang at me three times before I could hop out of the boat and allow it to leave. I used up so much energy on my leap, I didn't have the batteries left to try and kill it.

All I saw was some extra leaves and some water. Leaves don't bother me—they slow down my leak. I scooped out the water, and after I laid my snake catch kit on the bottom atop a sturdy burlap sack, I untied the stem, checked to make sure my little rock anchor was still under the back plank, stepped into the stern, eased down, and set one oar in its strut. I shoved off with a one-foot kick against the mooring, flipped around by poling off the bottom with the other oar, and aimed my bow straight across the middle of the Knee clearing and toward the Toe lane on the south side.

When I got to the middle of the Toe clearing, I stopped and watched my ripples run toward the edge, and I waited for the water to flatten into a mirror. A couple of weeks ago I had seen a very large rattler sunning along the edge. When my boat settled and quieted down, I could hear everything moving along the edges of the water. I heard only a bullfrog breathing. Now, as I turned slowly, all I saw were frogs, leaping off the sunny lily pads into the water.

I started to row again, but quietly, and slowly I circled along the bank. After I made a turn and a half, I heard a motorboat out on the river side of the blind. The boat went back and forth several times between the reeds and the triple overhang, then paused and puttered down to an idle.

A couple of minutes went by before the motor revved up to a fast putter again. Back and forth it zigzagged, moving slowly along the blind. The boat always stopped just short of the suck-mud bog. Someone was trying to find the hidden opening to the outlet and come through the blind. Such eagerness this far upriver was very unusual.

Who could it be? Minutes ticked by. Slowly, the current made me drift toward the outlet, almost close enough to touch the overhang. I dropped my oars into the water to check my drift. I had no intention of going out onto the river.

I stayed silent awhile longer. The boat made another close pass. Whoever it was still couldn't see the big hole right in front of him. I smiled to myself and waited a couple of minutes more just for the fun of it. I was tempted to laugh. Before I did burst and give myself away, I hollered over the blind, "Hello over there!"

"Hallo over yonder!" Skip Goodweather! My pulse speeded up, and I almost dropped my oars into the water. My mind began to race. Skip and Betsy had overpowered the sheriff, tied him up, maybe killed him, and were making a quick escape into Abernathy's Swamp!

Skip seemed to read my mind. "I know what you're

thinking, Bones!" he hollered through the blind when I didn't reply. I still didn't answer. Skip added, "I didn't rob the bank. I was framed. The sheriff believes my story. Are you still there, Bones?"

I needed more proof. Skip was saying what any escaping bank robber would say. I gave my oars another long, silent pull and sailed quietly and smoothly farther back, away from the blind.

"Bones!" Skip continued shouting. "The real bank robber set me up, like the others. That stack of bills from the Bank of Sun City was planted inside my car to put a scandal beside my family name, not to mention the trouble it's caused Betsy's folks. Someone's trying to ruin us for good here in town. Zeke didn't hold us, simply because we're honestly innocent. Can't you understand that?"

Just as I had thought yesterday—the money had been planted! Still, I had Skip Goodweather begging. All I could think about was the nasty, uppity way he had treated Toad Man and me on Saturday when he and Betsy had followed us down Orange Street, sneering and boasting and showing off, then spinning his wheels as they sped away, kicking up a spray of dust in our faces. And now Skip wasn't even smart enough to get inside the swamp by himself. I had good reason to ignore him. But I didn't want to hear him say later on that I had won the Rattlesnake Rodeo unfairly because I wouldn't let him inside Abernathy's Swamp. Skip would never admit that he was just too dumb to find his own way inside alone, and I would look bad. I thought about taking the chance. I was in no hurry though—I wanted him to crawl awhile longer. "You alone?" I called.

"Yeah!" Skip replied. "Who else do you 'spect I'd be bringing with me?"

I expected Betsy, maybe. "So, you're trying to get inside here?"

"Yeah." I could hear him sigh. "Where's the door to this darn thing?"

"What do you want inside here?"

"The same thing you're after," Skip said.

"Didn't you find anything big enough for you out along the river?" I asked.

Skip knew I was purposely delaying him, and he knew why, too. I was listening closely to the tone of his voice, paying close attention to the sound of his answers. But I was curious, too, to see the look on his face. "All the real big ones are inside there, and you know it, Bones," Skip replied. "That's how you ended up beating me last year. Abernathy's Swamp doesn't belong to you. And for the last time, I'm not a bank robber!"

I decided he sounded more like the same old nasty Skip than bank-robber Skip. "Aw, come on, Bones," he called. "You wouldn't be scared of me, now would you?"

"Can't you see a thing right in front of your face?" I said, giving in.

"I don't see nothing but a mess of leaves!" Skip shouted back.

95

I laughed and dropped my oars back into the water again to correct my drift toward the overhang. "You don't even see a limb that looks like it was trimmed a while back?" I asked.

"Yeah!"

"Lift it!"

"I'll be darned!" Skip lifted the limb and revved up his boat.

"Don't come through full throttle!" I warned him, and moved my boat over far enough just in case Skip didn't heed my advice. Of course he didn't. Before I was halfway through my sentence, Skip broke through the blind full speed. He came inside smashing aside limbs and spreading waves across the clearing. He listed me dangerously, and I would have capsized except that my last pull on the oars had sent me just far enough back and out of his way. What a fool he is, I thought. While my boat still rocked on his wake, I shouted over to him, "You almost swept me out of my boat!"

"I can see I didn't!" he yelled, grinning, and he cut his motor. Then we stared at one another.

For a long while I just stood straight up in my boat, letting my oars dangle over the side as I bobbed up and down on the waves and watched him. I'm tall for my age and pretty strong, even though I'm kind of skinny. Skip was heavier, but him being older didn't matter much. He didn't say anything else to me for a time either. His face looked more tired than his voice had sounded, and his skin was pale as a ghost. The dark circles under his eyes weren't only from lack of sleep. He surely hadn't shaved since his wedding yesterday, because his sharp jaw and square cheeks were full of stubble, but he had changed clothes. His fishing togs were a lot fresher than he was.

Letting each syllable fall out, I said, "Congratulations!" after what seemed like an eternity, still slowly rocking and rolling on his ripples.

"For what?" Skip asked. "Getting set up?"

I wasn't exactly disappointed over that. "Getting married."

"That's the least of my problems!"

"What do you mean?"

"Someone planted money in my car, then sent a special delivery note to the sheriff just to upset my wedding."

"A note?" It had a familiar ring.

"Yeah!" Skip said, with his face drawn in anger. "And marked 'urgent.' Zeke showed it to me." He slammed a fist into his left hand and the motion started his boat back to bobbing wildly again. "It told Zeke exactly where he could find the money."

"Wow!" I said, softly. I saw he was trying to show me how innocent he was. Him playing victim didn't exactly touch my heart. But why did he care what I thought?

"And you know," Skip added, "it even made special note of the fact that Betsy and I would leave town right after the wedding ceremony and have a splash of a honeymoon that would tour the eastern seaboard states, and end up at Niagara Falls. The part 'across the U. S. and Canadian border' was underlined."

I couldn't figure whether he was boasting or telling the truth. Knowing Skip, probably both, and the way he was watching me, there was another reason, too. Maybe he was thinking it was me who planted that money in his car? I would have loved to be the one. That he obviously realized. But Skip didn't really think I could be the bank robber—or did he? It was hard to tell what Skip really had on his mind, the way he kept looking at me.

"It's obvious whoever it is got the honeymoon information from our announcement in *The Sun City Herald*," Skip went on, still looking at me strangely. "The sheriff says at first he disregarded the crazy note. Then he got a telephone call shortly before he headed from his office to the church. Ooooooh, how I wish I knew who made that telephone call!" Skip smashed a fist into his left hand again.

"The whole town's paranoid," he continued. "Nobody trusts anybody anymore. Zeke's swamped with telephone calls, but most of 'em nothing but jokes. He's got a notepad full of what he calls 'leads.' Up to now every one of them leads to a dead end. Zeke's making mistakes right and left. He's never been anything more than an over-the-hill, overweight, parking-meter specialist anyway.

"I sure wish I could be sheriff for just one day!" Skip said seriously, watching for my reaction, because he had suddenly realized he was having a conversation with me for the first time ever and he'd already talked too much. He was so embarrassed, he abruptly switched subjects. "There should be some real big ones in here," he added.

"No need to be a sheriff to hunt for a bank robber," I said, and then regretted it. But Skip wasn't paying attention anymore to anything I said, because he had guessed, correctly, I was down at the Toe for a reason. I saw it in the sneaky way he kept watching me. I knew just what he was up to. So I eased down, sat back nonchalantly on my rear plank, grabbed my oars again, ignored him, and paddled my boat slowly around the edges. Every so often, I pretended I saw something interesting. Skip pretended he wasn't shadowing me, too. He knew I knew he was.

"You brought lunch?" I asked over my shoulder after a while of circling.

"Yup," Skip replied, chuckling, like we were close friends, as if we were together.

"I didn't," I lied. "I'm heading back home awhile to grab a quick bite."

"Perhaps I'll bump into you later," Skip said.

"Maybe so." I started paddling toward the water lane.

Skip followed me back through the passage to the Knee clearing, pretending he wasn't. He saw I wasn't headed home for lunch like I said, because instead of going toward the mooring, I continued across the clearing. And I didn't miss the fact he almost wrecked his boat in the dark lane when he rammed hard against a tree trunk he misgauged.

I couldn't outrun him in a clearing because his boat had a real powerful motor and I had to row, but I knew I could outmaneuver him in the dark lanes. I left him pretending to scout the edges of the Knee bank and turned my stem toward the north overhang, which was higher and easier to spot than the triple overhang back at the river, and shoved into the lane to the Middle. I poled halfway along it and stopped. At the midway point was a gap I could fit through between two wide cypresses. I settled my boat, angled backward through the gap, steadied my roll to kill the wake and waited for Skip to come looking for me.

In a few minutes Skip passed right by me without knowing it. I felt him coming even before I saw his bright headlight weaving in and out through the wall of trees, because Skip's trolling motor set off enough false current to rock me even behind the cypresses.

When Skip finally emerged out of the dark lane and into the open Middle clearing, he must have gotten a shock. And while he was busy trying to figure out whether I had drowned or headed up the next lane I poled out of the gap and streaked silently back to the mouth of the lane and, without stopping, straight across the Knee clearing, quickly through the next lane and back to the Toe.

I went straight to the spot where two weeks before I had seen that real big rattler. I found the little lime-rock cliff bare. So I decided to leave my boat and go up the rise to have a look.

I bedded my rock anchor in a soggy patch of fern, braced one foot flat on the bottom of the boat, and put my other foot down carefully because the lime-rock bank was mossy and damp. I brought my stem rope up with me. I was halfway out of my boat when Skip trolled out of the lane spreading waves.

I hadn't expected him so soon.

He caught me in a bad position. Getting out of the boat up against the lime-rock cliff was tricky enough without his choppy ripples rushing toward me. My boat began to rock against the bank, and then it started to move slowly away from the little cliff. I pulled the boat back a bit with my stem rope. But my legs started scissoring anyway.

"You thought you gave me the slip, didn't you, Bones!" Skip called to me, trolling around in wider and wider circles, creating more wake.

My legs scissored further, almost into a split. There were leeches in the water. I was having trouble getting my cliffside leg back to my boat, which rocked dangerously. Skip just laughed.

Suddenly I heard a small motor on the other side of the blind. Barely able to keep my balance, I turned just in time to see a sleek aluminum hull glide smoothly underneath the overhang and come into the Toe.

It was Fish and Mose Baker.

I seized the only chance I had left and jumped. It was a lucky leap. I was surprised when I didn't continue

101

straight through the bottom of my boat, but I still nearly took it under as I struggled to calm my dangerous list.

When Mose Baker saw what Skip was doing, he cut his motor and came to a coasting stop, and even though I had my hands full getting my boat back under control and saving the oars, I saw the meaningful, fiery look Mose Baker gave Skip. Skip froze.

It was all over in a second. Mose Baker never said a word. But Skip obviously remembered their big fight. And when Mose Baker felt that Skip had gotten the message, he started his motor again, revved up, and gunned it purposely, before guiding the narrow boat across the clearing and aiming it expertly into the dark mouth of the lane to the Knee.

By the time I even thought about speaking to them, Fish and Mose Baker were already inside the lane. Mose Baker cut his power and eased slowly through the passage as if he knew the swamp like an old-timer, in a way I have seen only my grandpa do. Then he and Fish quickly disappeared into the darkness.

After a long, still, deafening silence, enough time for Fish and Mose Baker to get some distance ahead of him, Skip made a tough-looking move like he was going after them. I knew Skip was just pretending, because he went about it too sluggishly, a very safe distance behind.

There was a way to find out. After Skip had slipped under the overhang, I let him troll inside the lane a ways before setting my oars. When Skip got swallowed up in the thick darkness, I waited until I couldn't hear his motor any longer; then I tailed him as he followed the Bakers. I went as deep as the Shoulder clearing, but I never found either of them. I circled around the bank several times before I found a freshly ripped lily pad floating at the mouth of the Head lane. They must've gone into the Head, I thought, and I wasn't about to follow anybody into there! I headed back to the Toe.

CHAPTER NINE

The big snake

AFTER THAT HOT, TENSE MONDAY morning not
even once in over a week and a half did I see
Skip nor the Bakers again. When they came out they'd
have had to pass through the Toe and see my boat. If
they did pass by, I didn't hear neither one of them.
Strange, because I stayed tied up along the Toe bank
pretty near the whole day, every day, for ten long days.

Inch by inch, I crept all over the rise of lime rock
where I had seen that big snake sunning. I knew better
than to expect to find some swirly tracks left behind
on the rocky surface. I was looking for a hole, a real
big one. I found a bunch of cracks, but none I saw
looked lived-in, not even the one that appeared to be
big enough for a large rattler's nest. I poked my noosed
broom handle inside of every good-sized hole I found,

but it always came out full of cobwebs, a spider's trap full of flies, often with a doodlebug crawling on it. It was already Friday, again. By the end of ten days I felt I had struck out. The rodeo was just a day away.

Then right where I had first started searching, in sight of the black water, not far from my boat, I saw off to one side, near a strange twirling fossil pattern, a spray of flat ferns. They led my eyes to a smooth oblong hole. It looked like it had a lodger. I raked aside the spray of ferns and probed cautiously around the mouth of the hole. I nudged the end of my broom handle a little ways inside to see if I could provoke a strike. It never came. So I decided to run my lemon test to see if anything was snoozing down deep.

I felt for one of the three fresh lemons I had stashed inside the burlap sack I carried on my left side, pushed through a belt loop next to my hunting-knife scabbard. Then I pulled out my knife and cut the lemon's nipple off. A lemon rolls better without a nipple. I scored the peeling where I had cut off the nipple and made a neat round hole dead center of the "X" cross. After I had drained mostly three quarters of the bitter juice out, watching it run slowly down the cliff to mix with the black water, I fished out of my sack the Coke bottle of gasoline I always kept tightly corked. Steadily, I poured the lemon half full and kneaded it gently to mix the gas and the rest of the lemon juice evenly. When the lemon pulp was thoroughly soaked, I tested my broom handle noose. It worked perfectly. I hooked the burlap sack back into my belt loop.

All was set. Even the muggy heat that had been hugging everything like a low fog for several weeks now had let up some this bright sunny Friday morning. Bending down, although I couldn't see it, or tell exactly from where its itchy sound was coming, I became aware of a happy cricket nearby. It was singing louder than all the rest. Maybe it was cheerful over the drop in the heavy heat that usually quickly dried up the morning dew. Though it led the cricket choir, a bullfrog's bark behind me overpowered it. Off to my left side I heard a lizard running away from something, and a frisky bird somewhere above fussing over a limb. A long stringy shadow tossed by some moss hanging from the tall cypresses partly shaded the hole, the rotten smell that alligators always give off passed by my nose suddenly, but I didn't let that cause my concentration to slip. Real easy, I lowered my "happy lemon" down to the oblong hole.

I had my gear ready. I waited a long while, but nothing rushed up. Not even a doodlebug. My lodger was out, or the hole had been just recently abandoned. I began to search in a widening circle for a possible new hole. I stepped slowly and lightly, looking for another low-lying fern, getting whiffs of the acidy rot of dead leaves that wafted up off the dark-gray damp ground of the swamp. A faint greenish taste was on my tongue, maybe because of the ferns everywhere.

I'm not afraid of any snake as long as I get to see it first. If I'm on level ground, I have no fear even of a sudden bite. My bibbed, steel-toe brogues kept my feet and shins safe from a low strike. Still, the rattle I heard behind me suddenly chilled my blood because the sound came from too high. I had to move fast. I forgot I was walking on damp, moldy lime rock, stepped forward too quickly, and I slipped in a fast skid down the far side of the cliff. Even though I hadn't laid eyes on the snake, the loud rattle made me think of a dragon. I grabbed for a crack in the lime rock to break my fall and left a trail of shallow dents in the soft rock where my fingers clawed it. I skinned my broom-handle hand raw, and the scratch brought blood. The noosed broom handle clattered on farther down the cliff ahead of me. Finally I broke my fall and snapped around. The snake was still shy of striking distance, but it quickly uncoiled, eased forward, coiled, and raised again. It was *big*. Slowly, I crawled backward, inching toward my noosed broom handle, groping for it blindly. I didn't dare take my eyes off the snake. Sweat ran all over me in rivers.

The snake wanted to fight. I wanted to let it go peacefully to its hole so I could see where it nested. I let it push me farther down the slope toward my noosed broom handle. When my heel finally struck the broom handle, I reached down quickly to grab it, sprang backward, and found an unmoldy patch of limestone where I was sure I wouldn't slip. I crouched in a position to use my broom handle like a club if I had to.

I didn't have many places to go, and the snake knew it, so I swung my broom handle to a whistle to drive it off.

It wouldn't move back an inch. I knew a strike was coming. I was looking for it. Twice the snake rose up, then eased back down, waiting to slide into a better position. It twirled into a coil again and raised slowly up, flicking its forked tongue out at me menacingly. The rattles it made sent chills all over me. The coal-black eyes watched every move I made. I'd never seen a snake so big or so stubborn.

I made another whistling pass, ready to swing right back. I knew I was breaking a rule by provoking it. My nerves just wouldn't let me be still. I had to let it know I could strike too.

Those coal-black eyes were looking for an opening, while that tail kept up a nervous, off-balancing, hypnotic rattle. The snake wove back and forth on its long pivot, drawing back slightly one moment, pausing the next. I waited, too, my broom handle cocked, holding my swing, watching it stare at me. The moment it drew its quickly flicking tongue back inside and hesitated just a fraction of a second too long was when it would launch its poisonous head toward me. I meant to shatter it as it flew through the air.

The seconds stretched. I had choked my noosed handle until my nerves wore raw. The spring inside me was wound far too tight. The snake was taking far too long to make its final move. And it appeared delighted to watch me sweat. It kept up its back-and-forth wave, as if greeting me and taunting me all at the same time, or perhaps—the thought suddenly hit me—looking for something.

I was standing on its hole. I can't say how I knew it. I was just suddenly aware it was underneath my boot. I moved my foot quickly. Would another giant snake come up out of the hole? I hardly moved six inches backward. I tried to step a couple of inches to the side as well. I was afraid if I moved any farther, or faster, I'd risk slipping again and tumble down the cliff, maybe falling into the water, maybe onto the other snake.

I fumbled around, as motionless as possible, searching blindly for a sure place to stand. I eased carefully over another slippery patch of moss before my sole held firm finally. Then slowly, I lifted my right foot and pulled it, inch by inch, back across the carpet of damp moss until I found another safe clump to stand upon.

After I surrendered its hole, the snake calmed down enough for me to pick my way slowly around it and down the cliff. It turned its head at the same pace as I moved, its eyes following me every inch. It stayed up in a pivot and didn't uncoil until I cleared the rise. My pulse didn't return to normal until I got back to my boat.

I couldn't just crawl into my boat and go away. I had to have the snake for the contest, and I couldn't go back and tell the story without the snake to prove it.

So I waited. I allowed it just enough time to settle comfortably into the hole while I got my wind back.

When I was rested, I took another lemon out of my burlap sack.

The snake was a big one, the biggest I'd ever seen. My burlap was strong enough to hold it, but still the drowse potion I gave it had to be potent. I tested my broom-handle noose again to be sure. I patted the burlap sack one more time. Then I began to walk lightly over the rise.

Every step I took was wary. I prayed the snake hadn't left its hole again while I had been getting ready. A few short steps from the hole I slowed to a crawl. I inched the rest of the way, expecting to hear a rattle any moment. A quick step away from its hole, I squeezed the lemon just enough to bring the gasoline up to the mouth of the score. Then quietly, but in haste, I bent over and swept my throwing arm out to just above the patch of fern, raked it aside with a flick, and just like I was delivering a package, I gently rolled the tricked lemon down the rattler's hole.

I heard him strike the lemon twice, quickly. The snake's trip up to the opening was swift. I stood back just in case it hadn't taken the full dose. By the time it got all of its long self outside the hole, it was drowsy and easy to handle. The coal-black evil eyes still stared menacingly at me, but the power to strike was gone. I looped its head in my noose and lifted it high so all of its tail would clear the sack.

The snake was bigger than I figured. The burlap bowed and my arm drooped. I didn't stand to admire my catch because I didn't want it to wake up before I got it out of the swamp. I choked the burlap closed, twisted it a turn, tied a thick cord around the neck, and wasted no time getting back over the cliff and down the rise.

I slipped, accidentally, and let the burlap brush the ground. The snake shifted its coil, a sleep reflex. I was much relieved when I got to my boat and could lower the burlap gently down into the bow. I reached back into the fern bunch for my rock anchor and stepped inside. Steadying my roll as best I could, I brought the stem rope behind me. The shove-off was the smoothest I could manage. It was the fastest trip I've ever made back to the Knee mooring.

Still half dizzy over what I'd just done, I walked away from the mooring, across the clearing, through the thick bush and briars, up the crooked rise of trail to my house, almost unaware of the weight I was carrying. I was through the gate, inside my yard, and standing before Bird and Ford before I realized it. They appeared to be expecting me and surely must have heard me groaning, but neither had come to open the gate for me. From a safe distance they followed me around to the back without uttering the slightest sound. They knew the snake I had inside my sack had to be real special. The way I was humped over I didn't need to brag.

I was afraid the noise might wake up my snake.

I didn't let myself relax until I got to the cage that goes back to the days—seventy years ago—when my grandpa used to compete in the rodeo. It has stood underneath the walnut tree next to the barn ever since he

111

built it. The wooden frame is stout. The door has a double latch and opens only from the top. It's covered with steel wire so fine, a flea would have a tough time getting out.

It wasn't so easy for me to straighten up quickly after being bent over for so long. Bird and Ford were no help. I stiff-armed the cage door up and over the hinges as fast as I could with my crampy left hand; then carefully I untied the cord I had wound tightly around the neck of the burlap. Quickly, I swung the heavy sack up over the rim of the cage and let the snake fall out by himself.

"Gee-ma-neety!" Bird whispered. "That's the biggest snake I've ever seen in my whole life."

"I hope so," I said, stretching the ache out of my arms.

"Bonapart, that thing could easily swallow you whole!" Ford was exaggerating, but not much. "Is it a boy or a girl?"

"Why don't you go inside there and have a look!" I said.

Ford backed up a couple steps when I cracked open the lid of the cage. Bird made the face she reserved for special occasions—like the Monday before last when I had brought home the news that Skip and Betsy had been found innocent of holding up the bank. Bird still doubted Betsy's innocence, because she still believed Doris's story of how Betsy stole the high school queen contest from Bird's idol, Jo Ann Grandberry. Bird had looked as if she'd jump up and fly away upon hearing

112

that, exactly the way she looked now, as my snake was showing signs of recovering.

"Close that thing, Bones!" Bird shouted. "He's coming to!"

I was sure I had a winner.

CHAPTER TEN

A rodeo that I'll never forget

L AST YEAR, MY MOTHER QUICKLY snatched away
the hundred-dollar prize I won and put it in the
bank—it was probably part of the holdup money the
bank robber had taken. Mom has shown the clipping
with my picture from the front page of *The Sun City
Herald* until it is almost shredded. Still, she hates
snakes. Bird and Ford can't stand snakes, either. But
they do like the carnival atmosphere at the rodeo, and
they are pleased to be associated with a winner.
Grandma thinks I'm evil. She's forgotten that Grandpa
was an eager participant, too, and that he brought a
trophy home seven times, although not always first
place. My father is neutral in public. His private opinion is What could be worse than a rattlesnake! even
though he has found worse things sitting atop a pile of

trash when he's popped the lid off a garbage can.

Sun City's Annual Rattlesnake Rodeo began over one hundred years ago as a simple good cause. Being so dangerous, rattlesnakes have hardly any natural predators, except for a few high-flying, low-diving big birds like the bald eagle, the hunter falcon, and the chicken hawk, but local sharpshooters wiped these out long ago for trophies to put over the fireplace. So the rattlesnake population often gets out of control. An annual roundup is one way to keep their numbers in check, because one bite from a pair of those poison fangs can put a victim in the graveyard before sundown. When rattlers overbreed, unprovoked attacks occur often. Campers, Scouts, and nature-loving hikers have had many close encounters with rattlers along the Old Spanish Trail.

Rattlers are jealous, territorial creatures. They roam about excitable if they get overcrowded, and they will fight quickly over turf they consider theirs. When they migrate, they're likely to take a shortcut across a freshly mowed lawn, boldly, in the daytime.

Six years ago, while I was in the second grade, a little three-year-old boy in Tallahassee was bitten by a rattler while he played in a sandbox in his own backyard, not even a football field's throw from the Florida State capitol building. The little boy's mother was reading the *Tallahassee Democrat* just a few feet away. She hadn't even heard the rattler crawl up.

The boy was saved only by a miracle. He was flown all the way over to the National Centers for Disease

Control in Atlanta, Georgia, courtesy of the governor's own private jet. After publicity pictures were taken, Governor Klaud Ferns personally organized the biggest rattlesnake rodeo in Florida's history. He touts the idea he started the first rodeo. It's a lie.

But it got "Fraud" Ferns elected twice. Now, in retirement, he is chairman of the Florida State Rattlesnake Association, a wing of the American Reptile Museum, whose headquarters are in the American Museum of Natural History in New York City. All record catches end up there, stuffed.

Every rattler caught gets milked after the judging and the raw venom is sent to the Centers for Disease Control to make a poison serum. After the milking, there is a rattlesnake fry. Only the losing rattlers end up in a frying pan, and there is always plenty of fried chicken for anyone who can't stomach rattler meat.

I could already feel the hundred-dollar prize money in my hand as I opened the lid to peep inside the cage to check on my big snake the next morning.

"You'd better go get dressed, Bonapart!" Ford called me from a safe distance behind. "Everybody is ready except for you."

"I've got to take out my snake," I said, without looking around. I heard Ford back up farther. "And I'm as dressed as I'm going to get."

"You be sure to tie the neck of that burlap real tight. If this one gets loose, he can have the truck!" my father said, holding the cage lid cracked for me so I could get my broom-handle noose inside.

All last week when I had been just hunting, and every day this week, too, all morning, right up until a couple of minutes before, everyone had been real chatty, discussing the latest talk that Toad Man and my father had picked up about the bank robbery while making their rounds. Hardly anybody could stop laughing over the latest joke about Skip and Betsy, who had been cleared but were still a hot topic because they had been the last to be framed. Now Bird, Ford, Grandma, and my mother rode clammed up and squeezed together like Vienna sausages inside the truck cab with my father. I rode in the back with my snake, alone. Bird and Ford kept glancing back through the window to see if I was eaten up yet.

I smiled back at them. I was just fine. There wasn't a cloud in the Saturday-morning sky, which was a real deep fairy-tale blue. I didn't mind the intense heat; my mind was on my big rattler and if my hunch was right, I'd probably get to talk to Doris, finally.

Long before we arrived, I heard the noise drifting off the high school campus football field from far away. My father guided our truck under the rodeo banner and turned left to the parking lot. Skip Goodweather's red convertible was the first car I saw.

We found a vacant spot in the third row, and everybody, except my father and me, got out and left the truck immediately. "You're not very popular today," my father said, and grinned.

"Just wait until I get that trophy," I said, "and the hundred-dollar prize money!"

117

Both of us grabbed a handful of burlap and lifted the sack. As we walked between the parked cars toward the entrance gate, which was all decorated with balloons, banners, and flags, I heard the rodeo band playing my favorite tune and my side got somehow lighter.

Zeke, looking more like Santa Claus than sheriff, was guarding the gate against crashers and robbers. The bank robber still hadn't been caught. I wondered if Miss Mildred Jones, the rodeo treasurer and ticket seller who hovered over the strongbox full of ticket money felt safer with him as her bodyguard. Though with her huge, round, sunburned, triple-chinned face, with a half ash and half cigarette poked in the middle, her wide, square shoulders, her big bosom, and her fat legs, she wasn't so weak herself. The thought made me smile. Zeke was looking straight at me, and saw me, but I'm sure it didn't occur to him what I was thinking. He gazed down at my sack while my father bought two entrance tickets with his free hand. "There's a monster rattler sleeping inside here, sheriff," I said.

The sheriff studied the contours of the burlap and said, "It sure looks that way to me, Bones. Welcome back to the rodeo, and good luck." Once Miss Mildred Jones moved her fat leg from across the gap, we passed through the gate.

The bleachers around the football field were packed. The more expensive seats, with cushions, arranged upon the playing field up to the measure-up circle at the fifty-yard line, were all full, too. Heads began to turn as people recognized me and started to whisper among themselves that I had arrived. A sea of eyes followed me as my father and I carried the burlap up the center aisle toward the judges' platform. I watched them all out of the corner of my eye. But like my father, who stepped like a soldier, I ignored them. I stared straight ahead of me, not forgetting I was carrying a live snake.

The rattler had begun to move about a bit because the midday August heat was beating down strong and the lack of fresh air in the sack had awakened him. My father, on his side, seemed fresh and cool, but I was sweating. Sweat began to run down my arm and drip onto the sack. Between the intense heat and the excitement, I had the feeling I was floating, as if we were walking in slow motion. The trip up to the judges' platform took forever.

Behind the dignitaries' row, I spotted the rest of my family beaming in my direction. (Now that they were a safe distance away, they looked proud to be associated with me.) Grandma sat like a twisted stone lady. My mother smiled under a set of tight pig-ringlet curls—Madame Baker's specialty, guaranteed to last a whole month, even in the summer. Bird waved to me, flapping her hands like an eagle taking flight. Ford yelled out my name over and over until my mother slapped him. Far away, up in the bleachers, my eye caught a glimpse of Doris applauding for me. She was the only one I saw clapping for me so overenthusiastically and so prematurely. I hadn't seen her since Skip's wedding, now almost two weeks, when she had had something "urgent" to tell me. My rattler moved suddenly again. I switched my mind back to it.

Half in a daze and wiping off sweat, I was assigned a box and a number. We poured my rattler out of the dark sack and into the box. The snake looked pleased to see some light and started to get sassy until I closed the lid. My father marched back to sit with my family while I took my place in the contestants' row. I sat almost at the end of the fifty-yard line. But it didn't matter. Last year's champion always got called first.

Toward the middle of the row Skip Goodweather leaned forward to catch my eye, mostly just to show me he was there. I already knew. He gave me a tough-guy look before suddenly straightening up again, and I saw why. I ignored him, and for the first time I noticed Mose Baker sitting along the row between us. He was staring straight ahead toward the platform, like he was thinking seriously about something. I hadn't seen either since that Monday morning, nearly two weeks now, when Skip had almost capsized my boat. I wondered what had happened between them when Skip had caught up with Mose—if he ever had. From the looks of things, Skip surely hadn't. Why had Mose Baker done that for me, that day, as if he were my big brother? I thought. Because he still hated Skip? Could it have been because I was black, like him, or did he just like to fight, as some people said? Maybe he liked to play the hero—he *was* in the Marines. What could I say to thank him? I couldn't help remembering nobody got close to Mose Baker without him first inviting them. As I was thinking, I felt someone staring at me. When I had focused better along the row, I saw it was Duck Tanner, sitting right next to Mose Baker. I pretended to wipe sweat off my forehead to break our gaze, and leaned slowly back on the warm metal of my folding chair to get out of his line of sight.

"Testin', testin', one-two-three," the mayor and master of ceremonies said into the mike. Holding his Purina Dog Chow clipboard to one side, the mayor glanced down at his watch, twisted around to check it against the official time clock set in the arch above him on the platform, turned back to face the audience, and straightened his cowboy hat. Any late contestants had until twelve o'clock—just five minutes—to show. Then the gate would be closed to all but spectators. Anyone bringing in a regulation-size specimen after the deadline would have to take his snake back home with him, or set it free, at or near the place of capture. The same goes for the ones that don't measure up. It's all in the rule book.

At the stroke of noon, the mayor tapped the mike and hollered into it, "Hear ye! Hear ye! Hear ye! All quiet please!" He paused for silence to sweep through the crowd, and cleared his throat loudly for the ones who ignored him the first time. When all was still, he said, "By the authority that's vested in me, I hereby now declare the Official One-hundredth Annual Sun City Rattlesnake Rodeo closed to further contestants and open to judging."

121

A long round of applause erupted among the expensive seats. A flood of hoots and whistles rained down from the bleachers. "Now let us all rise for the national anthem, which will be played for us by the Sun City Jubileers." We all rose in unison.

After the national anthem, usually the sheriff makes a long speech about law and order. This year, he wasn't asked to come up to the platform. The mayor read every line of his opening address; the applause began before he was finished. He cleared his throat, gaped a ticked-off look up over his clipboard, and walked away from the mike all red in the face, giving the show over to the judges.

"Contestant number one is last year's champion, Bonapart Russ. Come on up here, Bones!"

A burst of applause rang in my ears before I rose. It was a long walk up to the platform. My knees nearly buckled on me as I put a nervous foot up on the first rung of the steps.

"Don't forget your snake!"

In all the excitement I had bounded up the steps and onto the judging platform without my rattler. Embarrassed, I went back for my box. As I approached the steps again, I heard Ford shout out my name, and a loud bunch up in the bleachers began to chant in a chorus, "Viva Bones! Viva Bones! Viva Bones!"

I walked up the steps again with a wide smile. My rattler seemed to weigh a ton and the container boxes are built sturdy. Straining, I hoisted my box up onto the judges' table just inches from crushing their Purina

Dog Chow clipboards.

"On the floor, young man!" the arbiter judge whispered to me.

All the noise behind me had made me forget some of the procedure. I moved my box to the floor and got my broom-handle noose ready. Then I cracked the lid slightly to see how my snake was coiled. While it was stunned by the sudden light I looped it and inched it out of the box.

As I held my rattler up against the vertical measuring pole, it got heavier and the seconds appeared to stretch. It measured in at exactly six feet, half a foot longer than the snake I had won with last year.

"That's an awful lot of snake, young man!" the arbiter judge from Tallahassee said to me. The crowd didn't applaud me until I got my snake back inside the box.

I was only concerned about Skip's catch. I noticed Skip hadn't clapped for me when the crowd did. So when he was called up, I got a little nervous.

Skip grinned down at me from up on the platform just before he cracked open his box. His rattler measured six feet and just shy of another inch. Skip had beaten me. I knew I would never hear the end of it.

Skip wasn't a bit interested in the applause he got as he walked off the stage. He was too busy gazing down victoriously upon me with a cold, blue-eyed stare. Even after he was seated again, in our long row, Skip continued to lean forward turned my way. He flashed me a two-finger "V"-for-victory sign. I prayed silently somebody would beat him.

"Sergeant Mose Baker!" the arbiter judge called out next.

Mose Baker marched up the steps carrying his box with such ease, it was hard to tell anything about what was inside. But as he cracked open the lid of his box, all three judges moved back ever so subtly. And slowly out of Mose Baker's box came the biggest rattler I have ever seen or heard of. Even before all of the snake was out, I knew Mose Baker had topped Skip.

It was a record catch. Seven feet long! Mose Baker held the snake up against the vertical measuring pole so effortlessly, it could have been just a stuffed cloth boa. After all three judges had double-checked the seven-foot mark and its tail was let go, the snake drew up (a very normal reflex), and its middle was so big around and swollen, it looked as if Mose Baker had fed it just a short while before; maybe something as large as a tomcat. Of course he hadn't; the snake was just that big.

None of the judges lingered at the measuring pole long. Some quick scribbling upon their clipboards and they backed up in unison, slowly, to the edge of the stage and away from Mose Baker's snake box; then the arbiter judge hollered the boxing order. "You can put the specimen back inside now!" he said.

A few people in the crowd stood up to get a better look. Mose Baker held his snake up higher to oblige them. In a jiffy every spectator in the entire stadium was standing, all ooing like owls. Mose Baker's name was buzzing among the huge crowd, but he himself wasn't showing much emotion. Standing stiff in his Marines uniform, a row of medals glittering across his chest, he resembled a general with a riding crop—only the crop was alive, and starting to wiggle about. While he was holding his snake up in the air, I saw a curious look on Mose Baker's face. It was half delighted and half mean, as if by winning the contest, he'd finally gotten even with everybody he most disliked—all those who'd been nasty to Fish—in one stroke.

"Baker, put that thing back inside!" one of the local judges yelled.

Mose Baker was in no hurry. He seemed to be delaying on purpose, playing a dangerous game with such a poisonous snake amid a big noisy crowd, seeing the snake was already excited and getting friskier. What's he up to? I wondered. He's already won. What more could he want?

"Put that thing down, Baker!"

Then somehow, the snake's head slipped out of the noose before Mose Baker could get it back to the box.

The football field emptied.

CHAPTER ELEVEN

After the stampede

D URING ALL THE WILD commotion Mose Baker's snake got clean away. Hissing mad, ready to challenge anybody who tried to stop it, the snake wiggled off across the emptying football field. Its stomach was so big, the snake didn't move as fast as a smaller one could have. Catching it would have been an easy job. The reason nobody dared—not even one of us experienced catchers, who were used to cornering angry snakes—was because the snake wasn't the real danger: Getting trampled was. The snake was confused too. Several times it raised its head, looking for a way out; then it must've smelled water, I guess. Last I saw of it, Mose Baker's snake was heading down toward the reed bed next to river.

I hung around to see what would happen to Mose.

Since his snake was gone, Mose Baker got disqualified. Patting down his ruffled hair, the arbiter judge from Tallahassee called him over and gave him a real nervous lecture. It ended with Mose Baker being banned from competing in any future roundups. The bitter, squinty, satisfied look I saw on Mose Baker's face when he heard this said a lot. He'd probably had it in his head to do this all along, I figured, whether he won or not—probably the reason, I noticed now, I didn't see Fish and Madame Baker among the rodeo crowd. The crowd was full of enough people Mose Baker hated to pull such a stunt. He didn't seem at all displeased as he left.

And he left behind a mess. Folding chairs were strewn every which way. Empty paper cups, Coke bottles, and beer cans—some still leaking out the last drops—popcorn, ladies' and men's hats, babies' caps, one carriage, several suit jackets, umbrellas, and walking canes littered the ground, and loose balloons were everywhere. I spotted the mayor's cowboy hat, tilting, ready to fall off the judging platform. The Purina Dog Chow clipboards belonging to the judges and all the rodeo's statistics looked hit by a windstorm. I even saw an abandoned pair of crutches. Some lady had ripped off her gold necklace as she fled. I looked a little closer in the short grass. The tiny brooch attached to the gold chain was a trifle cracked.

The wild flight disrupted the rodeo some. A trickle of curious people did come back, slowly—mostly high up in the bleachers first. Then, bit by bit, the rest of the crowd started to come back, though they stayed in a jumpy mood for a while. Folks sort of stayed on their feet, milling about the judges' platform, ready to run if necessary. Every so often a heckler yelled out he saw Mose Baker's snake coming back to get his trophy. So most heads were always bent toward the river. The jumpiness in the air was hard to damper until the judges gathered up their clipboards, got all their statistics back together, and began to take control again. The arbiter judge from Tallahassee faltered up and stuttered into the mike, "Er, ah, folks, I don't think that snake is coming back amongst us since from the looks of it, it had just eaten! Like the old fisherman says, 'Don't tell me no tales about the big one that got away!'"

His joke wasn't that funny, but it calmed the regular Sun City crowd. All the tourists had gotten into their cars and vanished. Although no one else's snake got away—a few containers got knocked over during the stampede, but the sturdy wood took the tumble and the iron latches held—my folks had had enough. My father had rushed them home in our truck when Grandma complained of sharp pains in her heart region. My mother's curls drooped. Bird and Ford were very pleased to say good-bye to me. I stuck around and prayed somebody else would top Skip.

Nobody did. It was the very first time in my life I've ever found myself rooting for a member of Duck Tanner's crew to come out on top of anything.

Skip won. I was declared runner-up. Duck Tanner got third prize and walked off, cursing, to join his cronies.

When I had to watch Skip posing for *The Sun City Herald*'s photographer with a snake that I and everybody else knew was really nothing but a runner-up, my heart sank. Skip gloated, and hugged the champ's trophy and the hundred-dollar check like he was the real winner. Didn't Mose Baker realize he had thrown the contest away? Didn't he see he had let Skip win? He did hate Skip, didn't he? Could it have been that he didn't care anything about the hundred-dollar prize? I couldn't see why not. A hundred dollars is a lot of money! Skip sure didn't need it. Was Mose Baker so full of hate he couldn't see straight? Or was he really that clumsy?

Normally I like to watch the losers get milked, sliced up, and fried. Then I usually "flirt with the exotic," as some folks say, just as a dare, by nibbling on a hard-fried cube of fresh rattler meat dipped in a spicy condiment. I prefer Louisiana Tabasco hot sauce, myself. Now I opted not to eat anything. My stomach was crawling after watching Skip's champ act. He brushed up against me purposely as I was about to leave the rodeo. Betsy was with him. Skip waved his champion's trophy under my nose, tapped his larger cup to my smaller runner-up one, and said, "Cheers!" I saw in his eyes he knew he wasn't the real winner, just a runner-up like me. I was itching to tell him the real winner was somewhere down by the river.

"And where's the champ?" It was Mr. Pete Goodweather's voice I heard. Skip's father was calling him, almost directly behind me. "I'd like to buy a round for the champ!"

"See ya 'round, Bonapart," Skip said, winked, and walked off with a broad, false smile. I purposely didn't turn around. But suddenly I got a poke in my ribs from the back.

"Aren't you eating, Bones?" Toad Man ducked around to face me, nibbling on a greasy drumstick instead of a fried rattler cube.

"I'm not hungry and I was just leaving."

"Don't look so sad," he said between bites. "A cheap aluminum cup and a measly hundred dollars ain't the only prize around, if you know what I mean. . . ." Toad Man's eyes searched my face for signs I was interested in the subject he was hinting about.

"I think I'm hungry!" I needed to get away from him as quick as I could.

"Plenty of fried chicken left. Um treating," he said, following me. And trying to dodge him, I walked right into Doris.

"Did you forget I had to talk to you, Bonapart?" she asked.

"I've been trying to get to you since the wedding, but somehow I always get held up," I said, looking directly at Toad Man to place the blame on him.

"Not by me!" Toad Man said.

"Then excuse me?" I said.

130

"You're excused!"

I walked with Doris over to the bleachers. After she carefully checked underneath for Mose Baker's snake, Doris sat up on the second row. I sat down on the first because Doris has a strong crush on me and likes to show off. Toad Man was watching us.

Doris has got the blackest hair, which she always wears parted in two braided ponytails; the smoothest dark-chocolate skin; a round nose and lips the color of ripe plums she prefers to cover with too-loud cherry-red lipstick. She tries to compensate for the fact that she wears glasses. Doris is a little heavy, too. Still, she's cute, though I've never told her so, straight out. She wears the lipstick when her father's not around—her mother is dead. Doris once kissed me in the school hallway after I came in third place in a contest, smearing my cheeks and my collar. I couldn't get all the lipstick off, so my mother saw it and raised an eyebrow because as it turns out, Doris uses the same noticeable cherry-red color as Mrs. Baby Doll Long. This happened around the same time as the incident of Toad Man's unsigned letter. I hadn't known what to say to my mother to explain, and my saying nothing put a wondering look on her face. So when Doris was gussied up, I watched out. In a flash, she'll behave real grown-up in public. Since Doris will have nothing to do with snakes, she had come to the rodeo for only one reason—other than the one she gave—to show off. When I saw her start blinking her almond eyes like a giraffe, long lashes fluttering while she hesitated coyly,

I turned quickly away from her.

I found myself looking at Skip and his father, who were just beginning a loud celebration over at one of the refreshment bars. And they were drawing a large crowd of well-wishers. Finally, Doris said, taking my mind off Skip a moment, "I'm the model student cashier at the Piggly Wiggly supermarket for the month of August."

"Oh, congratulations!" I said, turning back to her like I was interested.

"It's no big deal," Doris said, feigning modesty. "I've got the worst cash register on the checkout line and they chose me for the hottest month. I was sponsored by the model student pilot program, not because I was the president of the seventh-grade class last term, and not because of the straight A's I got either, but because I was the seventh-grade representative on the queen committee and I caught Betsy's best friend, Dolly Overton, stuffing the ballot box with Betsy's name. I'm not stupid; it's nothing but a bribe to try and shut me up. I can't back out, either, because my father is so proud that I was chosen."

Just like I'd figured. I'd heard most of it before. Doris never got tired of telling the story of how Betsy had stolen the school queen contest last year from Jo Ann Grandberry, Doris's idol.

To distract her I said, "Still it must feel real great to have your fingers in all that money all day long."

"What money? Everybody shops with checks, or on credit!"

132

"But the bank has opened up again," I said.

"Yeah, but the bank robber hasn't been caught yet," Doris said, "and nobody wants to walk around town with too much paper money in their pockets these days. It's taking a real risk, you know."

"Is this all you wanted to tell me about?"

"No. I had something else in mind," Doris said, hesitating again, a moment too long for me, gazing down at me starry-eyed, her lashes blinking, acting romantic, her brown eyes magnified by her glasses.

I wasn't in the mood. It was hot and I had lost the rattlesnake contest to Skip, after all my hard work. I didn't hear much of what she said next. I looked across the football field to the river. Seeing all the junk folks had left behind after the panic, loose balloons strewn everywhere, made me think about Mose Baker, which made me think about Fish.

One Fourth of July, Fish stole Mrs. Riley's bloomers off her clothesline, put them high up on a long pole and paraded them around town like they were a flag. Skip had told him to do it. Old lady Riley wanted to kill Fish. I remembered well what happened once when Skip sent Fish over to the funeral parlor with a fishing pole and live bait and told him to go after undertaker T. L. Hooker's expensive goldfish in his precious front lawn wading pool. Fish almost ended up in a casket!

There were a lot of pranks played on Fish, though, that Skip had nothing to do with; but his were the ones most remembered.

Fish is also credited with doing a lot of things he didn't do.

Take Mrs. Crawley's marble birdbath. There is no proof Fish slaughtered her birds. It could've been Mr. Smarty, Mr. Baxter's nasty cat. Mrs. Crawley insists they were poisoned first, but Mr. Smarty sure couldn't do that.

And who killed the evil Mr. Smarty?

Anybody could've killed Mr. Smarty, really.

Who dug up his remains and put them in the Crawleys' garbage can? (My father found the corpse.) Anyone could've done that too. Maybe.

However, I know personally who painted Mayor Rowland's two black lawn jockeys white last Halloween night. . . .

"Bones, are you listening to me?" I heard Doris say. She was beating me on my back. "What I really wanted to tell you is that I saw who pinned that dollar bill on our clothesline."

"You what?" I turned around to face her and stared directly into Doris' blinking almond eyes. "You're kidding!"

"Nope," she said. "That's what I wanted to tell you the other day. My father's sick of hearing me. But I'll never forget that moment as long as I live."

"Who was it?"

"A tall man wearing a funny-looking pig mask," Doris said.

"Did you recognize who he was?"

"Like I've already repeated a thousand times to the

134

sheriff," Doris said, *"no!"*

"Why not?"

"Because I wear glasses. This pair I have on should've been replaced a long time ago. You know I hate wearing these things. They give me whopper headaches sometimes. Visions too. Most times, I see double unless I close one eye, and seeing a two-legged pig in my backyard next to our clothesline ranked right up there with hallucinating."

I nodded.

"I tried to blink him away," Doris went on. "When I opened my eyes again, the pig was still there. Well, I made the connection between the bank robbery and that dollar bill he was pinning to our clothesline, and I realized my eyes weren't just acting up on me again.

"I tried to focus on him better, but he was moving so fast it was hard for me to make him out clearly. Just a fuzzy-looking shape fading into a blob was all I saw, a blob slowly splitting into two people, both of 'em running down toward the river. I see real doubly far off."

Doris was sure drawing out this story as much as she could, I thought. Reminded me of Toad Man. I got up to get out of the hot afternoon sun. Doris followed me, not pausing even for a second, almost tripping as she climbed down off the bleachers. "I ran to the living room. My father was sleeping, slumped across the couch, and he got mad at me for waking him up. Once he did finally start to listen to me—him still sleepy-eyed 'n' all—right in the middle of me talking to him,

135

our telephone rang. Now you'd think he'd let the phone ring awhile until I got finished with what I had to say," she said with a pout. "It *was* more important! But not my father. He grabbed for the telephone and put a finger up for me to shush."

The refreshment stand where Toad Man was standing was doing less business and there was more shade, but I chose the next one although it was closer to Skip and his crowd of noisemakers, and I asked Doris to please lower her voice. "Well," Doris said, almost whispering, which seemed to draw more attention to us, "since he was *hello*ing into the telephone and didn't seem interested, I went back to the kitchen to make sure I wasn't just daydreaming.

"The man in the pig mask was gone. But the money was still there. When my father finally wandered back to the kitchen, he told me the person on the telephone just hung up. Real funny, huh? I pointed to the money. He came and stood beside me, almost like he'd been hypnotized. He couldn't say a word.

"Once he came out of shock, he got the screen door unlatched. Then, in one big hurry, he beat me out the door to the yard to get a better look, up close. He didn't have to warn me not to touch it. I wasn't stupid. I knew just what was up from reading the newspaper. While he circled the clothesline, wondering out loud what to do next, someone knocked on our front door.

"It was the sheriff. He already knew it was there!"

"All this crazy mess happened just shortly before Toad Man and I walked by?" I asked.

136

"Uh-huh," Doris said, and added, "but that's not half as strange as what happened downtown the next day at that wedding."

I couldn't figure out whether Doris meant the wedding itself, or the money found afterward in Skip's car. I asked, "Then you're the only one who's seen the man in the pig mask close up?"

"Except for Betsy, while she was getting robbed," Doris said with a smug look on her face.

"And you got no idea who he was, black or white?"

"I told you he was too fuzzy!"

"Short or tall?" I asked.

"Tall. That much I can say for sure."

CHAPTER TWELVE

The unexpected customer at the barbershop

W HEN I TOLD DORIS I WAS UPSET over losing to
Skip—by less than half an inch!—and
wanted to just be alone for a while, it was partly the
truth. I had something else on my mind, more than her
story about seeing a tall, fuzzy man in a pig mask pinning money on her clothesline. I wasn't in a mood for
company, so I cut behind the bleachers to dodge Toad
Man; but even after looping wide, when I curved back
to the river road leading home, I found him waiting for
me. I didn't say a word, and for once he sort of got the
message. It was about time. I kept watching him from
a squint out of the corner of my right eye. I saw him
looking curiously over at me occasionally. I didn't let
on.

In the road out front of his house, I paused near his

rotting gate. He had let it fall right off the hinges without fixing it. I didn't look up to say good-bye and started walking again. I took the shortcut by the city dump, then crossed Satan's Pasture.

When I got home, I went straight to my room and shut myself inside.

I share the room with Ford, who came to look in on me. I ignored him, too. He got the message quicker than Toad Man did. I don't remember when night fell Saturday night, or when Ford came to bed.

Sunday I slept. I left my room only to eat.

Monday I got up early and didn't stay for breakfast. Mom probably took my wandering off without saying a word as disappointment over losing the rodeo. And it was, mostly. The whole truth is I was going to town because my mind was on Mose Baker.

I knew I couldn't just walk up to him and start a conversation. Nobody got that close to Long Mose Baker. So for a while after I got to town I just hung around the landing out front of Joe's Barbershop along Riverside Lane. I spent so much time pretending I was fixing the leak in my boat, I nearly got a heat stroke.

Around ten o'clock I saw my chance. I spotted Mose Baker and Fish coming out of Dish Water Alley. They turned up Riverside Lane toward me. I was sure they'd go into the pool room, but instead they went to the barbershop.

Odd, I thought. Madame Baker, being a hairdresser herself, usually did all the barbering for her family. I stepped out of my boat in a hurry, left it bobbing, raced up the plank, and dashed for the barbershop as if I was late for a haircut. When I walked through the door right behind them, Joe, the barber, was starting to give another one of his famous speeches and funny demonstrations to his waiting customers. The place was roaring with laughter. Suddenly, all heads turned. The laughing dried up. Faces froze. Nobody wanted Mose Baker to think any of the laughter was directed at him, and especially not at Fish.

Mose and Fish sat down. Mose Baker tried a smile. After a long, stretched moment, the frozen air melted some. I took the vacant chair right next to Fish and started to watch Mose on the sly while he and everybody else pretended to turn all their attention back to Joe's amusing demonstration. "And this is how I'll treat anybody I catch attempting to slip some dirty money under my door!"

Old man Pool was seated in the barber chair. He was reclined comfortably, all lathered up from his Adam's apple to the low-hanging circles below his horn-browed eyes, waiting for his weekly shave to begin. Joe had talked for so long, old man Pool had fallen asleep waiting. So Joe grabbed the opportunity to use old man Pool as his model while he dozed under the mountain of foam.

Joe held old man Pool's nose pinched up between his thumb and forefinger while he cocked his straight razor ready to cut under old man Pool's vulnerable chin. He was aiming at the jugular vein to show everybody where he would slice when old man Pool woke

140

up suddenly, breathed a soap bubble up through the thick layer of lather, and asked, "Just what in the world's going on here, Joe?"

"I'm not finished yet, Mr. Pool!" Joe said, caught by surprise.

"Any fool can see that, Joe!" Mr. Pool coughed through the mountain of shaving lather. "But what's taking you so long today?"

The loud laughter drowned out Joe's reply. He cut short his funny demonstration and finally started to work. As Joe made a first razor cut and the long sweeping stroke chopping off old man Pool's tough beard made a rough scratching sound, I reached over and rapped Fish on his shoulder to cover my sneaking a closer look at Mose. "Hello there, Fish," I said, squinting, and grinned.

"Hallo, Bones!" Fish thundered back to me, giving me his usual sad, watery smile. For a moment as he stared back at me, I sank down into his flat moist eyes, feeling sorry for him, like I always do.

Although very busy scraping old man Pool's wire beard, Joe's eyes never missed a thing. He paused in mid stroke, grunted, cleared his throat, and said, "Can anybody hazard a guess as to who's this clever bank robber making the whole town hair-triggered? Everybody in town is so jumpy. *(Scrape, scrape.)* No one trusts their friends anymore. People are afraid to hang their clothes out on a line to dry. The Laundromat's doing a booming business. Already this morning, those poor overworked washing machines have broken

141

down twice." Joe walked around to the other side of old man Pool. "Overton's Hardware Store has sold out of padlocks because everybody feels the need to lock their mailboxes. First time I ever recall anyone locking a car door in Sun City before, and every last front door in town is bolted. Back doors stay latched. Even in this heat *(scrape)* most folks keep their windows shut tight. Everybody's double-checking window screens for holes and gaps." He looked up and waved the razor at us. "Innocent bypassers getting themselves yelled at, threatened like dangerous trespassers! Probably the very first time in history that nobody wants to receive an unexpected monetary windfall. Hee, hee, hee," Joe chuckled. "Anybody got any fresh ideas?"

He didn't pose his question to anyone in particular, but nobody was fooled. Joe was aiming at Long Mose Baker. Getting the message, all the regular customers stayed quiet. Mose ignored Joe's bait. Very politely he opened up the pages of a just-out copy of *The Sun City Herald*. I noticed he spied on everybody from behind it.

On the front page was an article on the rattlesnake rodeo. A picture of the wild stampede was staring at me. I wasn't in it. But there was an unhappy-looking snap of me below, and under it a caption saying "Runner-up." I cut my eyes away from the shot of Skip.

When Mose Baker didn't bite Joe's bait, and nobody else spoke up, I said, "Most likely it was an out-of-towner, Barber Joe. Folks in Sun City don't do such things."

"Oh, I beg your pardon, young man!" old man Pool

said up through the circle of foam still around his mouth. "Things are changing very quickly these days. There's a new breed coming out. Gutsy, not afraid of nothing. Just take a good long look at those lumber-mill strikers, bold and rowdy, no respect for law and order—this sort of foreign Communist influence didn't occur a short time ago, bank robberies neither. Now look! Not only is the bank robber not caught, he's still among us, who knows who, and giving out very embarrassing gifts whenever the mood hits him."

"Just my point," Joe said, still busy shaping up old man Pool's mustache. His back was now to Mose Baker, so Joe finally got up the nerve to speak to him directly since he didn't have to look him in the face. "Sergeant Baker, were you 'round when the bank got held up?"

Slowly, Mose Baker peeped up over *The Sun City Herald*, flicked a dust speck off his ironed and starched Marine Corps uniform, and replied, quite nonchalantly, "In fact, I arrived the very same afternoon."

"Then what do you think of our little scandal?"

"Probably some bored college boy with a wild imagination," Mose replied. "Perhaps some smart aleck who's seen too many late movies."

"Ummmmm . . . I never thought of that," Joe said. "It does resemble a movie, all right. I'm sure the sheriff hasn't thought of that angle neither. A movie freak! Maybe somebody ought to write the sheriff a note saying so."

"The sheriff's got more notes than he can handle already," I said, elbowing Fish on the sly so I could sneak another fast look at Mose Baker.

He caught me watching him.

"Howdy there, Mr. Runner-Up!" Mose Baker said to me, folding his newspaper and gazing straight into my eyes.

"Hey, Sarge!" I said, realizing I had been caught.

"Just why haven't you finished up yet, Joe?" old man Pool asked.

"I'm done now, Mr. Pool," Joe said, and started snickering. As he swabbed old man Pool off with a hot towel, Joe added, in a loud whisper, "Shall I dab on a little cologne just in case you decide to take Widow Riley out to dinner tonight?"

"Don't bother yourself, Joe," old man Pool barked. As he climbed slowly down out of Joe's barber chair, he gave Barber Joe a long, hard stare and said, "And my private life is my business!"

Quickly, Barber Joe switched subjects. Looking over his glasses, he asked, "Who's up next?"

Not counting the regulars who came in every day just to gossip, he had finished with everybody sitting in the barbershop, except for me. From the tone of his voice it was obvious Joe wasn't sure whether the Bakers had come for haircuts. Mose Baker looked up to signal it was his turn, even though he really didn't need one. His military flat-top looked fresh. Joe touched it up anyway, and he was very careful about it. Fish needed a good straight line because Madame Baker was much better at women's hair. She had always done a messy job of Fish's head. It was the cause of many nasty jokes.

"You're up next, Bones!" Barber Joe beckoned me, obviously glad to be finished with the Bakers.

He had caught me by surprise. I hadn't come inside the barbershop to get a haircut. I'd had other plans for the money in my pocket. But I'd sat there for so long, it would look real suspicious if I didn't get a trim myself. Slowly, I climbed up into the barber chair, surprised to see Mose Baker and Fish sit back down. "Just a little off the top and sides," I said as Barber Joe twirled the cover over my chest.

While getting a haircut I didn't need, and worrying about the extra expense leaving me short and listening to old man Pool snore over in the corner (he was one of the regulars who always came to gossip, catch a few winks, and of course read the newspaper, free), I was also trying to figure out why Mose Baker and Fish would linger in the barbershop. Gradually, I became aware that Mose was observing me.

After a few minutes, Barber Joe said, "It was an easy job this time, Bones." He smiled at me while taking my money. "You're early this month! Saw you were in a hurry. Got a hot date, or something?"

"I'm just about," I answered short, thinking of my wasted money.

"Then you won't mind having a couple of games next door with Fish and me?" The voice came from behind Mose Baker's newspaper and took me by surprise.

145

Not only was Mose Baker normally stingy with his words, the air around him didn't exactly attract people too close to him. He surely has never sent out any verbal invitations, as far as I could remember. But now bitter-faced Mose Baker was actually asking me to play a couple of games of pool—with him and Fish. Even though I'd come into town looking for Mose Baker, it was hard for me to believe my ears. "Since you're just 'about,' as you say."

I wondered if it had anything to do with my jostling Fish earlier. Maybe he knew if anybody could figure out he'd let his snake go on purpose, it was me. "Oh, okay," I replied.

As I stepped down from the high chair, I landed a fake punch to Fish's muscular middle.

"I'm, er, warnin' you, Bones—pow!" Fish landed a real one in my stomach. I almost doubled over.

"You've got to pull that punch, Fish," I said. "See? Like this!"

His second one was softer. I gave him a fake one to the jaw. Fish put a soft one to my jaw. Then I slapped his palm and said, "Friends. Give me five. The war is over!" Thinking, That's enough.

"Friends. Gimme five. The war's over!" Fish echoed me loudly.

It must've looked real strange, us leaving the barbershop together and looping next door to the pool room like three lifelong pals. I could feel Mose Baker watching how I handled Fish.

146

"Eight ball please you?" Mose Baker asked, as he racked up the balls.

"Fine by me." I sized up a pool cue and chalked it.

"Want to bet?"

"Not with a soldier!"

Mose Baker actually chuckled. Squinting up at me while he was still bent over the table, ready to lift the triangle off the balls, he said, haltingly, as if he had caught himself chuckling without really meaning to, "Oh. Just joking."

"Flip you to start?" I asked.

"Heads," he called.

"You lose!" I called back, after a fast flip.

"You're fast, and maybe sneaky." He chuckled again. "Break!"

"Watch this, Fish!" I hollered across the table to the bench, where Fish sat nursing his sad smile with his eyes fixed on me. I put the cue ball on the point, aimed straight for the pivot ball and gave the bunch a good jar. The balls scattered evenly. Good thing we were playing by Sun City rules, instead of the official ones, or I'd have had to sink a ball on the break, not get to choose one if I didn't. "High balls," I called, and sank the thirteen in the far corner pocket. I bumped the eleven into the side pocket, chalked up again, and aimed for the nine but missed it.

Mose Baker appeared to be opening up a bit. He smiled at my wild shot and said, "Mmmmmm, strong start. A little practice and you'll be dangerous." He cued through a tight hole left in the crook of his dog

147

finger and over his thumb. Before he tapped the cue ball, Mose Baker twisted his head slightly and called, "Fish!"

Fish bolted up from the wall bench like a soldier snapping to an order. Mose looked a little embarrassed, but he covered it. "Watch your big brother's technique real close, and then I want you to come over here and do the same."

"Just watch me beat Bones!" Fish thundered.

"You wanna bet?" I said.

"You wanna bet!" Fish echoed. Mose gave him a sharp look, so Fish sat down quickly. While Mose was busy, I got another chance to observe him real good. He took his pool serious. Although he was cued up, set, and ready to shoot, he was in no hurry. He was figuring out every angle and probably where the balls were going to end up after he had hit them. I had no doubt his mind was as sharp as those angular bones on his square head showing through his Marine crewcut. Mose was so tall and smooth-looking, and had skin so ebony black, he resembled a real Watutsi—an angry, lanky, muscular one. Bent over the pool table now like he was, it was hard to tell how awfully tall Mose really was. Most of his long thick neck was hidden by his wide shoulders, because he was hunched over the pool table so low that his square brick chin almost touched the green felt. His big biceps strained the short-sleeved shirt of his Marines uniform almost to bursting. All of Mose's veins stood out, looking like crooked rivers winding over his muscular arms. His large hands squeezed the pool stick so hard, it appeared he wanted to choke it. I could barely see the beads of his eyes, he was squinting so tightly, just two tiny sparkles that seemed to twinkle off his dark skin. Fine specks of sweat had formed on the bridge of his nose, but nowhere else—a sign, many folks say, of a person who likes to fight.

Mose had always had a lightning-quick temper. Nobody had dared cross him since he squared off with Skip three years earlier.

Looking at him now, so serious, cool, and neat, I could see why Mose had gotten so far up in the Marines so fast. And I wasn't the only one in the smoky pool room watching him. Duck Tanner and his bunch of fake toughs were there, too, but I couldn't even hear them breathe. The two players at the next table had stopped shooting to look at us. Nobody was on the bench next to Fish—a wise move. Everybody sitting on the bench on the other side of the table next to us was gaping. The two back tables had no players. The benches behind them were full of regulars who always came by just to gossip, tell jokes, watch and whisper, criticizing anybody who happened to be playing at the time. Nobody said a word now. Mose ignored them, too. In the space of a few seconds he cleared the table of the low balls, leaving mine scattered alone. Mose called his shot: "Eight ball going into the corner pocket." Then he sank it.

"Let's do that again," I said. "That was just a warm-up."

149

"Okay," Mose Baker said, "but you're sure you don't prefer Fish?"

"Okay, but you sure you don't prefer Fish, Bones?" Fish echoed.

"Just one more time," I said.

"Just one mo' time."

I racked the balls. Mose Baker gave Fish another sharp look before he chalked up and broke. Mose chose the low balls. One by one he sank them all. He bumped the eight ball into a side pocket after a double bank.

And at the same instant the eight ball fell down the throat of the side pocket, Barber Joe poked his head inside of the pool room and yelled, "There's a live rattler running around loose inside Goodweather's Bar & Grill, and all the customers are clearing outta there real fast!"

I twisted quickly around the corner of the pool table and met Fish and Mose Baker at the door. We ran the whole four blocks without stopping, from Riverside Lane to Main Street, to the Bar & Grill, where a crowd had already gathered out front by the time we arrived. Apparently Mr. Pete Goodweather had been dozing in his favorite spot, out front on the wicker bench under the awning, when Skip looked up and saw a long rattler wiggling toward the lunch counter and the cash register, and yelled, *"SNAKE!"*

Safely outside, Mr. Pete had positioned himself at the plate-glass window and was peeping through the fish tank to try to see what was going on. His baseball cap was twisted around backward. His flip-up tinted lenses were up so he could better squeeze his nose to the plate-glass pane, and he clutched a dirty flyswatter to his heart as he reported out loud the happenings inside. Betsy was inside all alone. She had gotten caught in the kitchen during the wild panic.

"Betsy's made it atop the counter safely," Mr. Pete reported. "She's screaming her lungs out for nothing, though. The snake's all the way over on the other side now."

"Where's Skip gone off to in such a hurry?" asked a customer who was carrying his unfinished hamburger in his hands.

"Skip's gone home to bring back the snake-catch kit," Mr. Pete replied, without lifting his straining eyes from the glass pane. "You don't think we keep a thing like that inside the restaurant, do you?"

"Why don't you just let the sheriff shoot it?" another customer asked, still chewing. "He's standing right here!"

"And if the bullet went wild?" Mr. Pete turned and asked. "This here plate-glass window costs a fortune to replace. It's hooked onto the fish tank." He tapped the specially built window softly with his flyswatter. "No, no. Skip will be back in a jiffy."

"How'd a snake ever get inside there in the first place?" I asked.

"We haven't had time to figure that out yet." Mr. Pete whipped around and spat. "Probably through one of the air ducts in the back. I'll have to take a closer look when Skip gets here."

"And what would a rattlesnake be doing in the heart of town?" I wondered out loud.

"This is rattlesnake season," someone said.

"Maybe it's the same one that got loose at the rodeo the other day," someone else said, as a shoving match started up from behind.

"Folks, step aside, please!" Skip returned and began to force a path through the crowd. "Let me by!" Skip shouted and elbowed. "A dangerous rattlesnake's inside there and my wife is pregnant!"

Someone behind me sighed into my ear. I got a whiff of cheap perfume amid the crunch of sweating, musty bodies, and the sharp corner of a pair of eyeglasses scraped me in my back. I turned, and my lips almost brushed Doris's rougey cheeks.

"Hi, Bones," Doris whispered, jabbing me softly in my back with her elbow. "You heard that? Now everybody in town knows the real reason behind their hasty marriage. Can you see a snake inside there? I get nothing but a reflection on the lenses of my glasses."

I felt Mose Baker watching as Doris used the tightly squeezed crowd as an excuse to show off. Putting her sweaty perfumed hands on my shoulders, she used them to lift herself to her toes and then pretend she was trying to look through the fish tank. I turned back toward the window, a little embarrassed. "No, but Skip's inching up toward the cash register now," I said, my voice almost faltering. "No, no, no—it's probably under one of the booths. That's where Betsy is pointing to in between her screams. Yup, it's under a booth, all right. Skip's going over there now." Doris' hands slid off my shoulders when I leaned closer to the window to better peer through the fish tank.

Skip approached the booth real cautiously. Slowly, he teased the snake out of the dark corner and into the light. It inched out, rattling its tail madly. The rattler struck the loop twice before Skip could lure it far enough out into the clear. It coiled, rose, flicked out its dark forked tongue, and threatened to fight three more times before it lowered from its swinging pivot and showed any sign of weakening. Skip let it spend up its anger and tire before he attempted to put the noose around its neck.

Once Skip snared its neck, he didn't waste time. Betsy was still screaming her lungs out even though she was growing hoarse. Skip stiff-armed the snake up and walked at a real brisk pace straight for the front door with the loop frozen horizontally ahead of him. The snake drew up shorter and wiggled about wildly when Skip pushed open the door and the sunlight hit it. Skip didn't have to ask the crowd to move away from the door.

Quickly, Skip glided across the sidewalk to the curb, stepped over the gutter, and carried the rattler to the middle of Main Street, where Mr. Pete was waiting with a shovel. Then they both took turns beating the snake's brains out.

When the snake finally lay flattened, Betsy crept out of the restaurant to take her turn. She battered what

153

was left of the snake flatter than a pancake. Betsy didn't stop striking the weird-looking omelette splattered on the asphalt until Skip said, "That's enough, sugar. He's dead now!"

"That litty-bitty snake caused all that fuss?" Doris said loudly. And as snickers burst out in the crowd, Betsy turned to stare daggers back at Doris. Elbowing her way backward slowly through the crowd, Doris left Mose Baker, Fish, and me standing along the curb and went back to her cash register inside the Piggly Wiggly supermarket.

"There goes my lunch hour," the customer who was still munching on his hamburger said. "My boss ain't going to believe any of this!"

I was wondering, too. How had a snake been smart enough to wander right into the middle of town, in the daytime, avoided being seen or run over by anybody, and among all the other possible places just happened to pick out the Bar & Grill?

It sure wasn't the one that had gotten away at the rodeo on Saturday. Mose Baker's snake was much, much longer. But a blinding thought buzzed me suddenly. Could Mose Baker have caught a second snake, smaller, and kept it hidden to use later?

CHAPTER THIRTEEN

Mose Baker's story
& his pistol

THE MORE I THOUGHT ABOUT IT, the heat wave we were having this August was enough to drive even rattlers crazy. It could have made one bold enough to come into town—if it had rained too much and flooded them out. But it hadn't. Not a drop. So to me this was more than just a coincidence. I saw four possibilities. One: An angry customer could've planted it to get back at Skip or Mr. Pete. Two: An angry customer could have gotten Fish to do it. No. I had to rule that out. Mose was around. You couldn't pay no one to go near Fish now. Three: It didn't have to be a customer at all. A lot of folks dislike Skip. And Mr. Pete isn't the most popular man in town, either. Four: It was a fluke. Still, my mind wouldn't let go of the idea that it was most likely Mose Baker who had done it.

155

When the paper came out the next day, I saw the Goodweathers had somehow managed to convince the editor of *The Sun City Herald* not to print the snake story. Instead, there was a full-page ad touting the Bar & Grill's beefed-up menu at "newly reduced" prices. Down at the bottom of the page, "Air-Conditioned for Your Eating Pleasure" was underlined. Hamburgers were going for half price, the first order of french fries got thrown in for free, and one cole slaw, too. It looked like the Goodweathers expected a serious drop in business.

Those prices weren't bad, and I was looking for a way to find out if they had discovered who had planted the snake. I kind of liked the idea of Skip serving me. If I stroked his ego enough, and called him "Champ" to butter him up, Skip would open up and talk. He'd always been a sucker for flattery. I was dying to tell him that next year he wouldn't have to go all the way up to Abernathy's Swamp to find a snake. He could just as soon look for one inside the Bar & Grill.

But in order to do that I would have to go inside the restaurant. I wasn't about to give my money to the Goodweathers. Though they couldn't go that far with the money from a small Coke, I thought.

I grabbed an early snack and got to town a little before noon, careful to stay clear of the places where I knew Toad Man and my father would be collecting garbage. I found Mr. Pete at his usual spot, sitting on the wicker bench on the sidewalk and choking a flyswatter, ready to strike, fully awake. Although his brooding eyes were hidden by his flip-up shades and the sun-visor bill of his cap, I could see he was counting how many of his good friends went across the street to eat at the Rainbow Trout Room. No one was going inside the Bar & Grill.

Mr. Pete rested the back of his head on a soft pillow pushed up against the thick plate-glass window. With the fish tank behind him, the fish appeared to be swimming around his head. A fly buzzed past and he took a swat at it. He missed the fly and spotted me. He eyed me suspiciously as I walked toward the screen door to go inside. Maybe he remembered it was me who had popped him that sharp question about the snake yesterday, because he had turned around and found me standing behind him. He sure knew I knew how to handle snakes. I was wondering, again, if the rumor was true about him being the head of the Klan. "Good day," I called as I reached for the handle to the screen door.

"And howdy to you." Mr. Pete spoke back, not real friendly though, but like he was glad to see any customer at all, and just before my hand reached the handle, I heard Fish Baker call out my name.

I looked around. Up the sidewalk, I saw him standing out front of the Piggly Wiggly, waving to me. Looking my way, too, Mose Baker had his arms around Fish. Clearly Mose had told Fish to call me.

I let go of the screen-door handle, turned, and started to walk up the sidewalk toward them. I could feel Mr. Pete's eyes following me as I walked past his wicker bench and away from the Bar & Grill.

"Just the man I was hoping to see again!" Mose said to me as I got closer to them. I couldn't read his smile, but it was surely out of character for him. Fish mouthed me a rehearsed, "Howdy, Bones."

"Hi, y'all," I spoke back. "You really been looking for me?"

"Yup," Mose Baker said. "We saw your boat tied up down the plank out front of the barbershop. Good we caught you before you went into that . . . place." The bitter look in his eyes told me he was still a long way from being over his fight with Skip. "You sure know how to sniff out a bargain in a hurry," he said, pausing briefly.

I got his point, but I had my reasons and wasn't going to explain them to him, even though he had paid for our pool table yesterday.

"Have a nose for something more adventurous, maybe?" he continued. "Fish and I are just about to float downriver to do some pirate shopping. You comin'? Or you got something else more interesting to do?" Mose added, nodding toward the Piggly Wiggly, where he knew Doris was a cashier, and his tone made it obvious he remembered her showing off yesterday, with her hands all over my shoulders.

I wondered what Mose Baker meant by "pirate shopping," and what he was up to, acting again like he was my big brother. It felt strange, him getting palsy all of a sudden. Looking up at him, so tall his head almost touched the Piggly Wiggly's awning, I remembered the effect he'd had on Duck Tanner and his bunch in the pool room. The idea slowly came around to me that even Mose Baker might have a good side. "Interesting," I said, "but not in my boat. It leaks bad enough with just me."

"No problem! The one we're taking's got no leak. It's big enough even for four, and it's got a motor. So we can use our energy . . . for, er, other little things," Mose Baker said, and winked.

"Ummmmm!" I sighed, thinking of the way he'd said "other little things." It *had* to have been him who'd planted that snake in the Bar & Grill yesterday.

"Well, what's stopping us?" he added when he saw me hesitating.

"Nothing."

We turned off Main Street into Dish Water Alley, then over the railroad tracks to where Dish Water Alley continued to Riverside Lane. As Riverside Lane narrowed to a trail and we walked the riverbank, I counted three uncut lawns. It was easy to see Fish got no requests for dirty work while Mose Baker was home on leave.

Mose Baker had rented the very same narrow aluminum-hulled outboard from Old Rufus that he and Fish had used during the rattlesnake roundup. Mose and I climbed carefully inside; Fish jumped. Old Rufus was watching, but he didn't say anything. Mose Baker waited for us to settle; then he pulled the spring cord to start the outboard and it sputtered to life. Slowly, we eased away from the landing at Old Rufus' Bait & Tackle & Boats for Hire. Out in the middle of

159

the river Mose revved the little motor up past the usual putter. Old Rufus stood up the plank watching us, squinting his eyes like he was in pain himself. He never liked for anyone to strain his motors.

"Just how far downriver do you intend to go?" I asked.

"All the way to the end of the river!" Mose Baker answered, urging the little motor up even faster. I was perched on the forward plank, leaning into the wind. Fish sat in the middle with his mouth wide open, catching air. When the boat rose up in the water suddenly we both got swept backward.

"All the way down to the Gulf of Mexico?" I asked, to see if in the three years he had been away in the Marines he'd forgotten what was downriver.

"Nothin' to stop us!" Mose Baker squeezed harder on the gas.

"How're we going to get past the falls and shoot the rapids down at Springfield Junction in this flimsy thing?" I asked, gripping the boat.

"I've done it once already, you know!" Mose Baker said.

"Without a parachute?" I said, so he'd know I didn't believe him.

"Nope," Mose Baker snapped. "That time I was in a puffed-up, almost-bursting tire tube. The tire tube never did burst, but my head almost did." He shook his head. It looked hard as a rock.

"Sure you're not pulling my leg?"

"Watch out! The sergeant will pull your leg," Fish said suddenly.

"No, I'm not pulling your leg, Bones," Mose Baker said. "And ten years ago I did a lot more than just tug on mine. I cracked my shinbone against a hard rock that refused to move out of my way, and I had bumps the size of Texas all over my head." He shook his rock head again.

I didn't miss the fact that he had used my name for the first time.

"And the falls?" I asked. "Just how did you survive them?"

"Easy," Mose said, grinning. "I simply blanked out and didn't have them to worry about anymore. It's probably the stroke of luck that saved my life. I just went with the flow behind my lucky tire tube. Fortunate for me, an old watermelon farmer just the other side of the drop was standing there that exact moment admiring the rainbow. He saw me coming down the falls and fished me out in the nick of time."

"Fished 'm out 'n the nick o' time!"

"The old farmer told me later he pumped enough water out of my gills to irrigate his whole farm, almost. I remember he nearly finished crushing my rib cage too. My leg was broken. He set the bone himself, right there on the edge of his field. I fainted right back out from the terrible pain. When I finally woke up again, I was in Dr. Schultz's office with a cast on my leg and a lollipop in my hand. Seems I was instantly famous.

161

Everybody in town came by to get a good long look at me. The old farmer was the first one to autograph my cast." Mose sounded real proud.

"If you're thinking of trying it again, you can count me out," I said.

"Oh, not exactly," he said, "not e-e-exactly," shaking his head now like he was remembering real vividly just how he had managed to survive. "This time I'm stopping before the falls. Up to the rapids is far enough for me. I like to come down here sometimes, just to remind myself. There's the farm right over there," he pointed. "Oooh, what a miracle that was!"

Suddenly, I felt the pull of the rapids tugging at us, and I gripped the boat. Fish too. Moving fast, Mose Baker gave the tiller a sharp turn and the little motor a faster spin that sounded real weak to me. But it spun us around enough to point us away from the falls. And just in time Mose gave it another quick, halting burst that lurched us forward. The little motor struggled hard, with rock-headed Mose Baker smiling, as he angled us over toward the bank, then curved gradually, by inches it seemed, back upriver.

"A-a-almost too late!" I said. "A little further and we could've never stopped in time."

"Just testing my reflexes," Mose Baker said.

With a weak motor in this devilish current? I thought. The three of us were riding heavy, at good speed. The current was helping to push us. Around rocks water is always faster. It was like fighting to keep from sinking. Mose Baker liked to flirt with danger. I

162

started paying more attention to the river, since it looked like he wasn't. The bank was close but in fast water that's not what counts. The water wasn't deep but in such a rush it doesn't matter. Up the bank there was nothing around for a couple of miles except wild marsh to one side and more swampy woods behind the old farmer's few summer crops on the other. The falls drop off at a real hemmed-in spot. No place to prank.

He obviously got a kick out of making me a little nervous. Grinning, Mose skirted a rock too close for my liking as we pushed into the upriver current. Then holding a hand up to his mouth, almost bursting, he said, "Anybody wet?"

I knew what he was asking. Not about the water that had splashed in the boat. "I'm fine!" I said, though I was so busy worrying about the boat, I didn't have the time to think about the snake in the Bar & Grill, the robbery, or the reward.

Sad-faced, looking up at his big brother in awe, Fish snapped Mose Baker a salute, though with one hand still gripping the boat. "No, Sergeant. Um dry!" And Mose Baker nearly burst.

Fish made me laugh too. Snickering, we skimmed back upriver.

We were riding real deep in the water, so Mose Baker let up off the gas a little as we eased past Old Rufus'. Still the little red Evinrude whined, especially after all the work it had just done. Mose had made it toil to the limits of its tiny horsepower, much more work than it was used to doing, and the puffs of smoke

163

coming out of the exhaust made it obvious—if anybody was watching.

Old Rufus was bent over a broken motor, repairing it. We trolled by quiet enough to get past him. Mose Baker didn't mash on the gas again until we reached the curve that goosenecks before the Bottom. Old Rufus never saw us.

"Close!" Mose Baker said, laughing.

"You had me sweating awhile!" I said.

"You had me sweating awhile!"

We all snapped salutes to the River Boat as we sped by and didn't slow down anymore until we got all the way upriver to the swamp. Approaching the blind, teasing us, Mose Baker swung real close to the stand of reeds and the suck-mud bog. When he curved us around to the blind, I held up the hidden limb so we could skim under the overhang. As Mose Baker eased the skinny hull through the narrow outlet three birds spooked and flapped out of hiding.

They were bats!

"A bad sign," I said, as we came through the blind and poured out into the Toe clearing. "When bats fly out into the daylight, it means someone is going to die soon."

"Nothing but a witch's tale," Mose said.

"A witch's tale!" Fish's voice echoed across the pond and danced in the soft breeze up among the trees.

Mose Baker revved up suddenly and sent us lurching quickly across the clearing toward the passage. All

164

three of us turned to watch the bats loop back to the overhang to hide again. We didn't turn back around until we got near the dark water lane.

A real strong spray of bright light coming from the Knee clearing hit us in the face when we poured out of the dark entrance of the lane. "Not bad!" I said.

"Think you can do better?" Mose Baker asked.

"Not with a motor," I said. "But I can move my boat across the black water without making a sound and hardly leaving a ripple behind me."

Mose Baker twisted the throttle sharply again to give us a real quick burst of speed, jerking Fish and me backward, and in a flash we were coasting up against the old Knee mooring. *"Pirates out!"* Mose shouted. "But make no sudden or suspicious moves."

"Pirates out!" Fish parroted. "Nothin' sudden o' suspicious."

"Nobody's watching us so deep in the swamp," I said, and stepped up onto my old landing. Almost too late, I remembered it was weak. Quickly, I said, "Fish, watch out, the landing's weak!" But I caught him too late. Fish had already jumped up to the landing, and it was beginning to rock. The weak boards sagged under me, kissing the water. The ripples I made licked the boat, which now rubbed heavier against the mooring and made it shake even more. Still Fish didn't walk that lightly, making the old mooring rock worse, and I hadn't gotten to the end of the plank yet to put at least one foot down to safety. "Careful, Fish, or we'll all sink!"

165

"Fish!" Mose Baker called. "Walk softly."

"Yes, Sergeant!" Fish answered, and snapped around, rocking everything still more.

"Careful!" Mose Baker shouted, ending it with a tender, patient, big-brotherly look that made his shout seem less severe.

"Okay, Sarge."

I got to the end of the mooring and stepped down to some spongy grass. I knew Mose Baker was watching me behind all of his out-of-character happy-facing. I was watching him too. I gazed down at his reflection in the water as he tipped along the edge of the planks, appearing almost to burst holding down a giggle. If anybody else dared laugh at Fish this way, Mose Baker would surely tear them apart. Now he seemed to be urging me to laugh, too. I found myself wondering, again, just what he was up to.

As soon as he was off the end of the plank, Mose Baker began to fish around inside a pocket. He pulled out three finger-fishing lines and said, "Anyone for a throw out?"

So this is all he means by "pirate shopping," I thought, fishing without poles. He obviously had all of this already planned. The three fishing lines were sure no accident.

"*Fish!*" Fish said.

"Sounds good," I answered, still thinking. "But Fish, you got to shut up. There's not a thing worse than a big-mouth fisherman!"

"You shut up yourself!"

Mose Baker grinned and said, "Everybody shut up! As a sergeant, I'm the senior officer here."

Except for Mose Baker fanning at the mosquitoes, nobody said a word for at least a half hour. We caught enough palm-size perches for a good fry.

I was so hungry, I could've eaten the fish raw. Mose Baker cleared a spot to build a fire while Fish and I went to gather up some twigs dry enough to burn. In Abernathy's Swamp finding anything dry is a job. When we didn't find enough twigs, Fish and I went farther up the bank and broke off most of the first dead tree we found.

After a few Boy Scout tricks I knew myself, Mose Baker said, grinning, "The fire is hot. But you fellows aren't hungry, are you?"

"Just a bit," I said. My growling stomach had forgotten about the little snack I'd hurriedly eaten for lunch.

"Just a bit, Sarge."

My first fish went down so fast, my stomach hardly noticed it. I snapped up another one and quickly leaned it over the popping twigs. The fish sizzled loudly, dropping oil on the fire. I saw a scale Mose had missed as I twirled it. Sure was real good eating.

I hadn't noticed the time go by. The fire was beginning to fade, like the late-afternoon sun. The only sound left was Fish's bone sucking. Once Fish finally finished cleaning his bones, I could hear the water licking the boat down at the mooring. The marsh-rot smell usually rises gradually toward the evening, but today it wasn't all that strong. Mose Baker spat, a bone probably, and said, "Not half bad!" Then he burped loudly, sprawled backward, and it appeared he fell asleep. Fish and I stayed awake. We took turns watching one another awhile. Fish's attention span is short. Soon he turned to the water.

For a long while I felt like I was absolutely alone—even though I was sitting next to them—looking out over the pond and, like Fish, watching the sparkling dance of the ripples upon the black water. I always liked listening to the swamp, especially when there was hardly any sound left to listen to. When my eyes grew tired, I let myself sink slowly back upon some spongy grass. I felt the moistness of the ground through my shirt. It was damp on my back, though not chilly. I let my lazy eyes follow a large cloud moving slowly across the sky. The light began to change. Finally the cloud blocked out the sun.

I felt myself falling slowly into a sleep. I craned my neck around to have a last look over at Fish. The sparkles swaying on the black water had sucked him into their dance. His sad, flat, moist, dark eyes were glued on the pond.

I was half asleep. I hadn't noticed that Mose Baker wasn't asleep and didn't realize that for a long time he had been studying me as I watched Fish. When Mose spoke suddenly, I was startled.

"Bones, you see that old oak tree over there at the edge of the clearing?"

I nodded.

"When I was just two years old, not old enough to

168

remember much but a bottle, really—exactly nineteen years ago, the middle of August of 1952, the seventeenth to be specific—a black man was found dangling on a rope from that stout limb in the middle over there."

"You're kidding!" I said, turning over in the grass to face him, remembering suddenly that today was the seventeenth of August.

"Nope," Mose Baker said, real seriously. "It happened right here, on this very spot."

"Why haven't I heard about it?" I had heard some rumors.

"Oh," he sighed, "this swamp's got a lot of bad stories you've never heard about. Our town's got some secrets nobody dares talk about because everybody wants to forget. Most folks have already forgotten about it. Others've convinced themselves it never happened.

"Real life can get much like a dream sometimes—a nightmare if you ever get a streak of bad luck," he went on. Gradually his face began to look like the old Mose Baker again, real bitter, and sad too, now. "A bad story is something people try to hide. If they can't hide it, they hide from it. Let me tell you, Bones, that makes life confusing. It's hard to admit to something wrong. Oh, yes! I know that for myself."

"Why hasn't my father ever told me about this?"

"Maybe it's better he didn't," Mose Baker answered, shaking his head. "Proves my point, though. Your father didn't lie. He just didn't tell you this particular ugly story."

169

"Who did it?" I asked, thinking again about the rumors I'd often heard.

"The town," he answered. "Among them are a few that everybody pretends are our finest citizens. People you know, probably respect—even eat at their restaurants." He looked at me sharply. "Names aren't important."

I got the point, though I couldn't figure out why he was talking about this just now. Because of this being the seventeenth of August? I wanted him to keep talking, but I knew better than to urge him because I sensed his bitterness again now, and Mose was unpredictable.

Still, I asked, "Why'd they hang him?"

"They didn't hang him. They lynched him!"

Lynched! I knew what that meant. I'd read a story once, which my father got very uncomfortable discussing. "Why'd they do a horrible thing like that?" I asked.

"'Cause he was organizing and urging black people to vote," Mose answered dryly.

"That old oak tree there!" I said.

"That old mossy one right over there," he answered, pointing so there could be no mistake. "My mother brought me out here to show it to me when I got old enough to understand. Eight years ago. I was thirteen, just like you and Fish now."

I'd come past the old mossy oak almost every day since I was big enough to sit in a boat, surely hundreds upon hundreds of times. Looking at it now, trying to

170

picture a lynching, I thought, why would Madame
Baker go and do a thing like that? What did this have
to do with her? Who were those "people you know"
he'd mentioned? The "restaurant" he had hinted about
was crystal clear, especially after the way he'd behaved
earlier, calling me, deliberately stopping me just as I
was about to go inside the Bar & Grill. But who were
the others? How many were there? "The town," he
had said. I had so many questions, I didn't know
where to start! "Why didn't the sheriff do something?"
I asked.

Mose Baker didn't answer me.

"Nobody did a thing?"

He gave me a look that said, "You got a lot to
learn."

"Just who was this man?" I asked.

Mose Baker stared harder at me. I'd seen the look
before. Not on him. Other adults. The air got real
tense. The seconds wouldn't tick. I thought of apologizing, but I couldn't say, "I'm sorry I asked." That
sounded dumb. I knew I had to think of something
fast, because I saw I had asked the wrong question and
it didn't look as if he would ever answer me. I'd already opened my mouth. I don't remember what I was
about to say. But I never will forget his reply.

"My father!"

I was so shocked I couldn't say a word. "He wasn't
the only one," Mose said. "Just the last one—in this
swamp."

It was too awful to think about. I tried to think of

171

something else, but every time, my mind went right back to it. I kept going back and forth: from the old mossy oak tree to the bank robbery; from the old mossy oak tree to the disgusting Toad Man; from the old mossy tree to my losing the rattlesnake rodeo to Skip Goodweather; from Skip Goodweather to . . . I felt I would continue to do this for the rest of my life. Then I thought, My father always warned me about digging too much. I finally got myself calmed down enough to say, "I'm sorry."

"You got no need to be sorry if they aren't," Mose Baker said bitterly. I didn't have to ask who he meant.

This must be the real reason people stay out of Abernathy's Swamp, I thought. And now every time I have to come by this old tree—and I could hardly avoid it—I didn't want to think about it. Why was Mose telling me all this? Maybe he saw I was curious. Could be he was telling me because his mom had brought him out here when he was thirteen, like me now, and Mose saw it would be a waste of time telling Fish. Maybe he had another reason. I wasn't even sure I wanted to know.

Still, just how in the world was I supposed to go on living in this town, walking around and acting just like nothing had happened, and not let my feelings show? Was this why Skip Goodweather always acted the way he did? Mose interrupted my thoughts.

"At first they only burned a cross on our front lawn. Then a few days later they came to our house and took him away in the middle of the night. The Klan—all of

172

them wearing hoods, but my mother recognized some of the voices. Daddy yelled for Mom to go get the pistol. One of them grabbed her and held her. She was screaming, with me crying and clinging to her nightgown while they stuffed him into one of the cars they had waiting. It was the last time we saw him alive.

"She knew most of the cars," Mose Baker continued, his eyes glowing like hot coals now. "I know who every last one of them was," he added with a secret smile. He sighed. Then he abruptly changed subjects.

"Do you know when the first of the Abernathys got his grant of land—I mean the great-great-great-grandfather of all the Abernathys, who got the forty acres and a mule promised him and all ex-slaves after the Civil War? Old man Abernathy discovered his forty acres were this swamp and he got so mad that he was on his way to Washington, D.C., to shoot the president but John Wilkes Booth beat him to it!"

"That I do know!" I said, still looking at the oak tree.

"Do you also know how to shoot a forty-five?" Mose Baker asked.

"I've never had the chance," I said.

"You wanna try?" he asked with a sly grin. Then out of his fish-vest pocket he pulled a giant pistol.

"I'd like to."

"Fish!" Mose Baker called. Fish was still glued to the dancing black water. When Fish heard his name called, he snapped out of his trance and answered as if it were a roll call.

"Here!"

"Now watch the sergeant!" Mose Baker commanded, and quick as a cat, he rose up to a squat, bounced to his feet, stalked over to the edge of the pond like a soldier in combat, and took aim.

Far on the other side of the black water Mose Baker shot a giant bullfrog that was catching mosquitoes on a lily pad in the twilight.

The frog exploded.

Mose Baker hadn't even disturbed the lily pad. There wasn't a single ripple in the water around the edges. I said, "All soldiers shoot like you?" but I was thinking, He's real dangerous with that pistol.

"All those with a sharpshooter medal," he replied with a smile. "If either one o' you can do what I just did, he's got twenty bucks."

Fish jumped to try it, I think mostly to please his big brother. Fish almost used up a box of cartridges, always shooting wild, even when Mose steadied his hand. "Cease fire!" Mose shouted. "Good our country's safety don't depend on you. Bones!" he called. "Your turn."

I had changed my mind now about wanting to shoot Mose Baker's pistol. I wasn't worried someone in town might hear us. We were too far upriver to be heard all the way downriver to town, but my house was sure near enough. I knew how to handle that. If the subject came up, I'd just say I was in town, and hadn't heard a thing.

A part of me still wanted to shoot, but I could never

174

hold that heavy pistol straight after seeing Mose Baker kill that poor innocent frog, and my mind went back to the horrible thing that had happened at the old tree.

"It's too dark," I said. "I probably wouldn't hit a thing now."

"You're probably right," he said. "It would be a very sorry end for an expensive box of shells. It's time we headed back to town, anyway."

CHAPTER FOURTEEN

I'd forgotten who'd surely show up at the skating rink

MY FATHER KEEPS A PISTOL hidden in our truck behind the seat. He thinks I don't know about it. Toad Man carries one too, sometimes. He showed it to me once but has never let me touch it. Almost everyone in Sun City has one, whites as well as blacks, and it's no surprise to anyone if sometimes it happens to be in their pockets. Most people say they're for snakes, though they're not fooling anybody. How many people in Sun City ever really see snakes except at the rodeo and that's just once a year? So it was no big deal, really, that Mose Baker carried a pistol. It was the horrible story he'd told me that had me thinking.

We hardly talked on our way back downriver to town. Mose Baker changed moods fast. He went back to his normally bitter self, and he was watching me

176

again. I caught him at it several times. I was watching him on the sly, too, examining Fish's resemblance to him. They couldn't have had the same daddy because Mose's father had been lynched nineteen years ago. That meant Fish and Mose were only half brothers. Maybe that was another reason why Mose was always embarrassed by Fish, yet always ready to fight to defend him. I wanted to ask Mose more about that old mossy oak tree in the swamp, but he wasn't the kind of person to bother, and I'd found out why.

After seeing him shoot that frog with a hand so steady, I knew his clumsiness at the rodeo had to be just an act. And the way he could handle a boat, it was easy to see Mose was no butterfingers.

When he and Fish dropped me off by my boat, Mose gave me a terse "See you later, maybe?" that Fish repeated like a parrot. I hopped up to the landing and waved good-bye to them as they sped off to Old Rufus'. Mose Baker gave me the disturbing feeling he was more dangerous than I'd first figured. I wasn't sure I wanted to get too close to him. Still, he wasn't silly at all, like Toad Man. And he had a way about him that people sort of respected.

When I looked down, I found a surprise waiting for me. I'd left my leaky boat for so long, it was full of water. I bailed out just enough to keep it from sinking. I never like to get inside a motorboat. It makes me hate rowing, and I can't afford a motor. Wiping the heavy sweat off my face with my sleeve, I started up the landing.

177

I decided not to go home—especially after all that shooting—because it was family night at the skating rink. All of us got in for half price if we came together. It would be stupid for me to waste my energy rowing upriver against the current, getting more sweaty, and have to bathe before coming back to town. And I'd have to go past the old oak tree twice, in the dark because I probably would not make it home in time to catch my family before they left. I didn't want to have to stay home alone tonight. Waiting in town also gave me more time to figure out Mose Baker, and if I skated myself tired at the rink, in the middle of a crowd, I could fall asleep without thinking too much. I hoped my folks wouldn't forget my skates.

I hopped off the plank, hot, not interested in seeing anybody else for a while. Mose Baker's conversation was too strong on my mind. It was quite dark now and still so warm nobody was out on Riverside Lane, though I heard much loud laughing inside Joe's Barbershop and some boasting coming from the pool room. I slipped by and got into a fast gait, cut right through Dish Water Alley to get off Riverside Lane in a hurry, crossed the railroad tracks, turned left on Main Street, angling across, and took the shortcut over the little triangle of lawn of Confederacy Park to the old railroad station. Like I always do, just for a gibe, I gave a quick salute to the graycoat's statue as I walked by, and in a few shakes I was at the skating rink.

The waiting room of the old railroad station had been converted into a skating rink. The train doesn't stop in Sun City anymore—it just gives a whistle as it goes by. If you want to get on, you have to go to the next town up the line, the county seat. I sat down on the steps to think awhile.

Connecting Mose Baker's story to all the rumors I had already heard, all those whispers about Skip's father being part of the Klan were true. "Others," Mose Baker had said. Who else had been with Mr. Pete that night they had lynched Mose Baker's dad? I started silently counting off all the white men I figured were about Mr. Pete's age, and the next thing I was aware of was Doris standing in front of me holding her skates. Time had flown. "Are you going in with me tonight, Bones?" Doris asked as she sat down next to me.

"You know Tuesday night is family night, Doris," I said. "If I go in with my folks, I pay only half price."

"Then let's do a couple of doubles later," she suggested.

"Maybe a single double," I said with a grin. "You know I'm a freestyler."

"Something bothering you?"

"No."

An engine misfired up the street and I heard a familiar rattle. I was glad to see my father's truck come rumbling across the railroad tracks toward us. Doris got up and dashed away quickly when she saw my grandma inside the truck with the rest of my family. Doris can't stand Grandma's paralyzing stare. I went to meet the truck to see if they'd brought my skates.

Nobody was speaking. They were all angry at

179

Grandma, who pulls the same trick every Tuesday night. First she says she isn't coming. Then, just when everybody has piled into the truck and they're charging out the front gate, Grandma comes streaking out of the house like it's on fire, hollering, "Stop!"

"Always the same old problem," Bird said to me, looking back toward the truck cab at Grandma. As she jumped down ahead of Ford, Bird added, "And tonight, she's worse."

"Why so?"

"You mean you haven't heard? Old lady Riley is dead!" Ford said. I was surprised Doris hadn't mentioned it. I shook my head, recalling that while I'd been with Fish and Mose Baker in the boat, we'd seen those three bats fly out into the daylight.

"She died this afternoon," Bird continued, "and Grandma has been acting up ever since."

Grandma is afraid of dying in the house all alone. I think she often exaggerates her fear just to upset everybody, but old lady Riley's fresh passing sure didn't help matters none. So when I saw the looks, I just grabbed my skates without another word and went ahead to wait for everybody at the ticket window.

"Bones, you been in town all day?" my father asked as he paid for our tickets. I was just about to slip through the turnstile.

"Yup!" I said, turning. I could feel Mom watching me. "Why?"

"You didn't show up for supper and your mother heard some shooting in the swamp."

"Probably somebody fishing had to kill a snake," I said.

"According to her, this was too much shooting for a snake."

"Didn't hear a thing this far downriver," I said over my shoulder. "Ask Doris."

"Oh well, then," he said with a secret smile, taking it that I had been with Doris. I was glad he'd left it at that. I felt kind of guilty about the lie I'd told, so I turned around quickly and continued through the turnstile.

Doris, already making the rounds on the bumpy floor in her flat-footed style, waved over to me when we all got inside. As I got fastened up next to Grandma, I waved back to Doris and said to Grandma, who doesn't skate, "Why don't you buckle up and come on out?" just to try to make her smile, and to cheer myself up too.

It didn't work. "Florence Riley and me were class-mates." Grandma started recalling her past, with watery eyes, her glasses drooping down her nose. "Now that she's dead, I'm the last one of our crew."

I tried to think of someone around her age still alive. "There's still old man Pool left," I said.

"Why that slick little George Pool is nothing but a youngster pretending to be an old man," Grandma said, jerking her head sharply upward. "Nothing but a young brat compared to me and old Flo!"

I waited until Doris got to the other side of the rink before I cut out into the Tuesday-night traffic. I was the first one of my family out on the floor. I buzzed back around past my folks after I circled the rink doing a wide-legged Russian dive. Bird licked her tongue out at me. I ignored her and beckoned Ford to hurry up so I could teach him a few things. My mother is always quicker fastening up than my father. He doesn't admit it, but I know it's because my mother skates better than he does, and he doesn't want her to look at him when he first stands up on his wheels. In the turns, he's wobbly. Grandma is just a looker, but tonight she wasn't the least bit interested in watching. She sat on her "reserved" bench, stiff backed up against the wall, with her arms folded and a faraway stony stare like one of the sad pictures I've seen of Mrs. Mary McLeod Bethune.

The first hour is always devoted to flying singles, freestylers, show-offs, and the slowpokes who take time getting in the groove. Usually I like it best because I'm a freestyler. I almost never fly as fast as I could, but I'm no slowpoke like old man Pool either. Tonight, I had decided I'd go full out. I did a couple of real fast toe spins in the middle, made a complete split all the way down to the floor until my seams almost ripped, and rose without a hand touching the floor, something I'd never accomplished before; I leaped up to a fresh start, did a heel-to-heel circle, and got back into the flow a safe distance ahead of Doris, who I noticed was watching me, but I wasn't doing it for her.

The fast-rhythm music was ideal for a freestyler who wanted to show off a new routine, and the dimmed lights and the strobe made a practiced freestyler look like a real pro. I wasn't thinking about how I looked. Still, Bird said, "Skating wild like that, you going to break your neck one of these days, Bones!" with undisguised jealousy in her voice.

"You wish!" I shouted back, then edged on up ahead of her. I wasn't doing it to make her jealous tonight.

My mother finally eased my father out onto the floor. In order not to hurt his feelings, she kept her pace down to an old-folks crawl. Old man Pool was still the slowest poke of all. And he thought his advanced age gave him the right to ignore the announcer's call to clear the floor for doubles.

Behind me there was some loud cheering and hooting. I turned and saw Skip and Betsy come out onto the floor. Unlike his usual self, Skip didn't start out reckless. He's slowed down some since Betsy is going to be a mother, I thought, but I saw the thirst in Skip's wild eyes. I looked around a bit and there in the corner at the refreshment bar was Mr. Pete leading the cheers. I glared at him.

"Who're you going to couple with, Bonapart?" Skip asked, distracting me. I had slowed down so he and Betsy overtook me. I had just given Skip a sharp look he surely misunderstood when suddenly, in front of him and Betsy, I saw Tommy Shack cut in and skate over toward my sister. Bird, smiling all over, slowed down as Tommy approached. Now I knew who Bird had flipped out for.

Tommy lived across the river with his older brother,

Big Shack, in a place worse than the Bottom. Both his parents were dead. Tommy and Big Shack never had any water, lights, or working sanitation because they never paid their bills. Grizzly Big Shack was always in trouble, and Tommy was slowly learning his ways. I didn't want him around my sister. I sure couldn't see what Bird saw in him. Maybe it was the flashy new clothes Tommy wore these days. How'd he pay for them when they couldn't pay their bills?

Tommy was about the same height as me, though a half year younger. He always did need a haircut. His dark-brown face was long and bony, a pimple always sat on his boxer's nose, and there was an ugly scar over his brow that he had gotten in a fight in the Bottom. He skipped school when he felt like it, so he hadn't any friends except Tank, from the Bottom, who gave him that scar. Nobody else in town wanted to be around Tommy Shack until he suddenly started wearing new clothes.

My mother saw what was happening too. She left my father partnerless and sped to the rescue. Mother caught Ford from behind by the seat of his pants and launched him toward Bird. Ford was surprised to find himself picking up speed. Ford and Bird collided, but only Ford got upset. When Bird reached down to help him up and found herself with a partner, Tommy Shack had got the message. He skated off, his eyes glued on Bird, and sat down partnerless.

While I was distracted, Doris sneaked up behind me, grabbed hold of my hand, and pulled me away. My skates almost ran out from under me. "The announcer called partners," Doris said, smiling. I skated a little faster after I got my balance back, so Doris had to speed up or break her hold. "You're going faster than the music," Doris said to me.

I started to skate even faster. Curving, I saw the Bakers come inside. Mose Baker had brought Skinny Mabel Jefferson along. Seeing them together again reminded me of the way they danced at the Paradise Club, two and a half weeks ago, when Toad Man and I were there. After they had fastened up, Mose Baker waited for Doris and me to circle closer, then he cut in and guided Mabel alongside us, winked at me, and began to twirl Mabel into a few fancy figures he wasn't very good at. Doris and I had to slow down so as not to bump into them. Mose Baker was sure better at dancing than skating, I thought. Mabel was bad at both.

Fish and Madame Baker skated together. Fish was nearly always standing on his brakes, but he was steady enough—with the madame doing the guiding— to say, "Hey Bones, is that your girlfriend?" as they passed slowly by and moved to the outside. I knew Mose Baker had put Fish up to it, so I skated Doris up even with Mabel and Mose and locked eyes with him. I had thought we might smile over his joke, but the look in his eyes took me back to the old mossy oak tree in the swamp. I looked back over in Mose and Mabel's direction much longer than I should have, and I didn't notice the pileup building in front of us until I felt

185

Doris suddenly start backpedaling. Doris missed her brakes. In a panic, she let go of my hand and began to flap her arms in reverse like a falling angel. Instead of slowing down, she gained speed before doing a cartwheel in front of me.

I tried to stand on my brakes too, but I never got my toes cocked up high enough in time. Doris finished her tumble atop the pile of bodies. I crashed into her rear, the last to collapse on top.

The announcer, John Taller (a fan of Skip Goodweather) stopped the music, flicked on the bright lights, and hollered into the loudspeaker, "If anybody's hurt, I'll call the nurse!"

Skip and Betsy, who somehow had missed the pileup, skated over. Both did perfect toe stops. They appraised our wreck, smiled, and skated off, giggling, after I gave them both hard looks. The giggling didn't bother me. What I now knew to be true about Skip's dad did.

Nobody was really hurt, although the ones on the bottom of the pile were exaggerating, of course. As I brushed off my knees and raised my head, my eyes met a grinning Mr. Pete. Still sitting over at the refreshment bar, he was almost falling off his stool laughing. Some of his best friends had joined him now. Mr. Crawley, Mayor Rowland, Mr. Baxter, Mr. Overton, Mr. Miller, Mr. Bullers, Mr. Cotton, and Mr. Cutter, the owner of the bank, who seemed to have added more gray since the robbery. All these white men were around Mr. Pete's age—between forty-five and fifty—

except for Mr. Cotton and Mr. Cutter, who were both pushing toward sixty and showed it. Were all of them part of the Klan, too? I wondered. Where were they all this night nineteen years ago when Mose Baker's dad was lynched? Were they the "others" Mose Baker had referred to—all still walking around town as if nothing had happened? If not, they sure had to have known about it. And after all this time nothing had been done!

Then I remembered the way Mose Baker had stared at me when I had asked about the sheriff. Why hadn't Zeke done his job? Surely he knew! But Zeke closed his eyes to a lot of things. Then why hadn't Madame Baker gone higher up, to the federal government, for example? I'd have to find a way to ask Mose about that.

Skip had really misunderstood my sharp look, and blaming me for sailing her into the pileup, Doris limped off angry at me. Really I didn't mind.

Madame Baker's stepover style and her not watching where she was guiding Fish had apparently caused the accident. After the mountain of bodies lifted up off her, she hopped over the skate wall and sat on the bench beside Grandma, who sat unmoved by all the other onlookers' laughing, still with her faraway stony stare.

My folks, who had been in the pileup themselves, were already there next to Grandma, rubbing their bones. I was happy to see Madame Baker had taken Fish with her. Mose Baker stayed out with me.

"Much safer freestyling," I said, watching Skip and

Betsy leave the rink behind Mr. Pete and his cronies.

Mose Baker watched them too. "Then try and catch me," he said, distracting me.

I did, and kept up the pace until I winded him. In a few minutes I was looping by him twice for every lap he skated. Normally I'd feel great, with my family cheering me on each time I buzzed past (all except Bird). I didn't tonight.

I continued to loop the rink until the music stopped.

CHAPTER FIFTEEN

The pig mask

I DREAMED I WAS FLYING. Then my father suddenly jerked me down out of my cloud when he tickled my foot. "Come on, wake up, Bones!" he said, shaking my big toe. I opened my eyes. "Get dressed," my father continued, which cleared my head. I saw through the gap in the curtains the sun wasn't even up yet. It dawned on me Toad Man was out sick, or faking. So that's the reason he hadn't been at the rink last night, I thought. I had been able to dodge him for a long time. I should've known sooner or later he would make me pay. Perhaps he was jealous I had been spending so much time with the Bakers.

"What's wrong with Toad Man?" I asked, just for the sake of protesting.

"He says his stomach's been growling, paining, and

acting up the whole night. Says he woke up with the runs," my father said. "Let's make it snappy, Bones. It was already late when he walked over here to tell me how poorly he felt."

"Nothing was wrong with his feet?" I said.

My father didn't see my point.

I was glad we collected garbage on Doris' street before she rose; she didn't see me, but her father did. Reverend Black stuck his sleepy head out the back door to make sure we weren't robbers. He said, "Good morning," and quickly disappeared back inside his dark house like a bat. Later, as we picked up the Bakers' garbage, Mose, who was out gardening, waved.

Wednesday is a heavy garbage day. It was the day of the week my father allowed people to throw out small articles of unwanted furniture, if they liked. Some people exaggerated. If they did, we left the heavy stuff behind. Toad Man knew he was doing me dirty, and I hated him for it. My father and I made three runs back to the city dump before noon. By the time we worked our way into the center of town, it was hot; I was filthy and sweaty, and stunk of garbage. I had been lucky to miss Doris, but I wasn't so fortunate dodging Skip (the last person I wanted to see!), who I was hoping would not come out back of the Bar & Grill to watch me lug and empty his filthy garbage cans into our truck bed. I was wrong. Before I was halfway out of our truck, he poked his head out of the kitchen window. Skip didn't say anything smart because my dad was there, but he made a secret face to make fun of my appearance and

190

twisted his nose up in a sneaky way to say I stunk. And, as if that wasn't enough, he quickly came out the back door, stood there, the picture of comfort, and said, "See you again, Captain. . . ." Skip didn't have to add ". . . Garbage," but I knew he was thinking it. I felt like I'd explode. If Mr. Pete had showed up too now, I would've.

My father was slower than me getting out of the truck. I wondered how he felt, collecting the Goodweathers' garbage all these years. I was anxious, so I jumped out quickly, my heart thumping. I wanted to get the Bar & Grill over with real fast. Before my father got to his first can, I had already emptied one while Skip stood grinning at me. The way I felt about the Goodweathers now, picking up their garbage made me want to throw it in Skip's face.

I thought if I ignored him, he would go away. He didn't. Skip thought he was the champ. I was thinking, You chump! How much do you know about your own father?

Because Skip didn't take the hint and disappear, he gave me the chance to do something that I had been just dying to do for two days. "You had any more snakes inside there?"

It took him a moment to reply. "We don't have any more snakes in here," Skip said. I could almost hear his teeth grinding. "We discovered that little one we found was planted by someone. We know how. We don't know who did it—yet. We will find out. And when we do . . ."

191

Maybe he suspected I had planted it. "What will you do?" I asked.

Skip never answered. What will you do if it was Mose Baker? I had wanted to ask him, and couldn't. Usually, my father mistook my haste for enthusiasm, but not today. He knew how I felt about the rodeo—he didn't know that I had found out the truth about Mr. Pete.

Watching us both, my father cleared his throat and heaved the second can over the side of the truck bed to empty it. Afraid to come out and really do it, but aching to shout, "You murderers!" I sped back and popped the lid off the third can.

A rubber pig-face Halloween mask stared up at me.

"Dad! Come over here, quick!" I called.

My father is accustomed to having strange things pop up in garbage cans, so he didn't take me serious and he didn't hurry. The look on his face said he suspected me of pranking. I stayed right where I was. After a moment of widemouthed shock, he said to me, real calm, "Go get the sheriff. Be silent and quick about it."

Skip was coming closer to amuse himself as I sped off.

When I told the sheriff I was sure I had found the pig mask the bank robber had used, he catapulted from his comfortable chair and left his office walking behind me faster than I've ever seen him move.

It took us only a minute or so to get back to the Bar & Grill. Betsy had come out to join Skip and my father now, but it seemed Mr. Pete was away. All three stood gaping over the garbage can.

After Sheriff Zeke got a good long look at the pig mask, he looked up at Skip's face. Then he said, pointing, "Skip, can you explain to me how that thing got to be inside there?"

"I haven't got the foggiest idea, sheriff!"

"When did you put out this bit of garbage?"

"Last night after closing, before going over to the rink," Betsy answered for Skip, who was looking sideways at me. I knew he would never forgive me for finding the pig mask inside his garbage can.

"Somebody planted that thing here!" Skip spat out finally, as he turned back to face the sheriff. "That's obvious!" I knew he suspected I had planted the snake. Was Skip suggesting I had planted the mask?

The sheriff looked doubtful and grunted loudly.

"What do I have to do?" Skip said. "Lock up my garbage cans?"

"If you do, I'll need a key. Otherwise, you're responsible for dumping your own garbage," my father said.

"Perhaps that's not the best solution," Skip said quickly.

I had to sign as a witness who had found evidence. My father signed after my name since I'm a minor. Skip got written up in the sheriff's report as a two-time suspect, found in possession of, or near, circumstantial evidence, and was given another warning not to leave town before the crime was solved.

Before letting him go, the sheriff all of a sudden

193

asked Skip a very surprising question. "You aren't by any chance one of those mourners who's been filing past old lady Riley's casket over at Hooker's Funeral Home, now, are you, Goodweather?" It appeared at first to be a joke.

"Why would I?" Skip asked gruffly. "She's no kin of mine."

"Earlier I got a call from the undertaker. He insisted I come over to the funeral home right away. You know what I saw there? An old dead black lady lying in her casket holding a fifty-dollar bill in her hand, a bill from the very same batch as the holdup money. As sure as heck someone put it there!"

The sheriff's question didn't trap Skip, but the insinuation did make him madder. It was the first time I'd been in a laughing mood all day, but I didn't let myself laugh, for Skip was boiling red now. I hardly stopped smiling the whole afternoon. For the rest of the day, at each stop we made, we found someone lingering at every garbage can. The robber's gloves and dark glasses hadn't been found yet. Some people were just double-checking to make sure. Most people wanted to hear about how I found the pig mask in Skip's garbage can. It seems I had become instantly famous.

And somehow, even lying suffering upon his sickbed, Toad Man heard the news. While we were making our last drop for the day, he rushed over to the city dump. "You recover real fast, Toad Man!" I said. I gave him a look he understood and continued kicking the last stray bits of garbage off the back of our truck.

"I'll be fit for work tomorrow," he said.

"Did you figure out what was wrong with your stomach?"

"It came on like a flash and went away after a while in a blink," Toad Man replied without meeting my eyes.

"You should watch what you eat," my father advised him. "But all's well that ends well. Bones did a good job today. See you tomorrow, then." My father looked over at me and winked, because we both understood that Toad Man had been faking again.

It was one of those moments when I could have asked my father just about anything. I had been waiting for it the whole day. But my chance to ask him about the Baker story slipped away because I couldn't do it with Toad Man around. He has never been one to know when to leave. I could see in his eyes he wished he'd been working so he could have found the pig mask.

I wondered why the sheriff didn't think the pig mask was enough evidence to lock Skip up. Seemed enough to me.

CHAPTER SIXTEEN

The arrest

NEXT MORNING, I HEARD TOAD MAN whistling softly on the back porch while he waited for my father to get up and come out to go to work. The thick dawn darkness I saw outside through the gap in the curtains told me just how eager he was. It was still a while before I heard my father step softly past my room and go out the back door to meet him. When he did, I smiled and went back to sleep.

As usual, after breakfast I dodged my mother, ducking out the back door to the edge of the yard, where I slipped up to my hideout high in the top of the pecan tree and sprawled inside my hammock. I hadn't been up here since that day, almost three weeks ago, when I saw Fish loping toward me with a note from Toad Man. As I rocked from side to side, the top branches swaying in rhythm with me, I was thinking, Did Skip hate old lady Riley enough to put that fifty-dollar bill in her casket? Who would want to insult an old black lady's corpse? I knew a lot of folks in Sun City, both black and white (none were the Goodweathers), who had gone to visit her secretly for her root-medicine cures. Some to have hoodoo spells cast. Maybe one of them was the bank robber, who had an illness she hadn't cured. Maybe she'd made it worse. Who? I thought. Then suddenly I spotted Fish Baker.

I climbed down and hurried out to meet him.

Not with a message from Toad Man this time. "The sergeant wants you, Bones," Fish mouthed to me when I met him on the trail.

I saluted Fish. He snapped a stiff salute back to me and turned around to follow me back across Satan's Pasture.

We took the fork of trail winding past the city dump because my boat was still in town. That worked out just fine for me, since doubling back around the marsh to the mooring would take us too close to my house and right past my mother's sharp eyes. And because that field was lying fallow this year, she'd certainly see me with Fish Baker who was, as usual, wearing his favorite loud red shirt.

Just before we got to the dump, I saw someone who looked suspiciously like Tommy Shack dodge behind a mound of garbage. I waited until Fish and I edged right up to the smelly pile before I shouted out, "You're a long way from home, Tommy Shack!"

197

He didn't answer me. I was sure I heard a tin can fall behind the pile. No breeze blew. The air was hot and still. "If you don't come out right now, I'll come back there to get you!"

Tommy rose up quickly and walked out slowly, looking back at something hidden behind the mound. And he wouldn't look me directly in the eye.

"You can come out now too, Bird!" I hollered over the mound of garbage.

Bird started pleading even before she showed her face. "Please, Bones, don't go tell Momma. We were just talking, that's all. I swear it!" Bird said, rising slowly, then broke into tears and ran off toward home.

Itching to grab him, I watched him looking at Fish. Tommy realized he was outnumbered, but the way he kept fingering his pocket, I suspected he might have a knife. Or was he bluffing to show me he was tough and wouldn't run? Who'd he think he was?

It happened very fast. I went for him, aiming to catch him with his hand still inside his pocket. Fish was between us, slightly, so maybe in my haste I knocked Fish's arm into Tommy. But the way Fish already had his hand raised—seeing as how the blow shook Tommy, stung his jaw, and cut his lip, bringing blood—maybe Fish was going to hit Tommy for me. Maybe it was just a reflex, like the day I threw Fish a fake punch in Joe's Barbershop and he sent me a real one back, not realizing, at first, I was just playing with him.

Seeing the blood, I stopped. Though I bumped into Tommy, sort of, before I did stop. I wasn't going to double-team him, but that must have been what he thought. Backing off from Fish, a vengeful look in his eyes and wiping his bloody mouth on his shirt sleeve, Tommy vanished.

I let him go. I knew where I could find him.

Mose Baker was waiting for us at the door of the pool room. When he saw Fish and me, he puffed up his chest and rubbed his hands together to let me know he was looking for some action. His smile was so wide, I saw all of his white teeth. The sun sparkled off the double row of medals strung across the breast of his uniform.

Still panting, because he had run and we hadn't, and standing real boldly right next to Mose was Tommy Shack.

Tommy's guts surprised me. As I got closer, he started making faces, provoking and taunting me with dirty grins. I couldn't take him laughing at me. I went over. Tommy puckered up his lips and made a kissing sound when I brushed past him close enough to feel him breathe. He grinned at my back, making that kissing sound at me again, to remind me he'd kissed my sister at the city dump. It was worse than a dare. I made another attempt to pass, and suddenly I heard his brother, Big Shack, inside the pool room almost ripping up the carpet because he had just lost a game. I should have known Big Shack would be inside.

"You got no right to chase me, Bonapart," Tommy said.

"Now listen here, fellows . . ." Mose Baker said.

"You got no right to kiss my sister," I said. "My mother doesn't approve of you, and me neither."

"Cut this out!" Mose Baker said, louder.

"I suppose your mother approves of you kissing Doris Black then," Tommy said, grinning nastily, and he made that kissing sound again.

"That's enough now!" Mose Baker said with a slightly deeper voice.

"I'll get you one day," I whispered right into Tommy's taunting face. "Big Shack won't always be around to help you."

"Say it louder!"

I couldn't resist grabbing him by his collar.

"Big Shack!" Tommy cried out as I began to squeeze and his neck swelled up over his collar.

I heard Big Shack's bear feet drag along the floor and his asthma breath scratching his throat as he threw down his pool stick and began stalking toward the door. I fully intended to choke Tommy before Big Shack got to me. When Big Shack reached the door, Fish, who had been standing behind me, suddenly blocked him. I thought surely he would take Fish on. Big Shack's last Thursday in one piece, I said to myself. But Big Shack had no trouble seeing the sergeant's puffed-up chest over Fish's shoulder, and he didn't miss the meaning of the double row of medals strung across Mose Baker's Marines uniform.

"I said that's enough, Bones!" Mose ordered me like I was a soldier under his command. "I asked you here to play pool, not make war. Save some of that energy for the game. And that's an order!"

I released Tommy and he fled again, the coward. Big Shack didn't flee, though afterward he scratched on almost all of his pool shots and swore loudly every time he scraped the felt when he missed the cue ball with his trembling stick. It seems Mose Baker's nearness made him lose his concentration.

My game got better. I changed my breaking style. I scattered the balls more evenly, making it more difficult for Mose to clear the table in one unbroken run. Even though he still won the game, Mose couldn't take me for granted anymore. Skating rings around him Tuesday night at the rink had given me confidence.

The next game, although it was his break, I almost got lucky and beat him. He scratched on the eight ball, twice before he finally sank it. "Ugh, I got distracted," Mose Baker said as an excuse. I didn't see what could've distracted him suddenly, unless he had something besides pool on his mind.

Then the following game, when it was again my break, I shoved hard and sent the cue ball crashing into the crowd at a good angle. The kiss I got was sharp, like a gun fired. I had given the cue ball good speed. The spread I got was a breaker's dream. I saw the look in Mose Baker's eyes. Fortunately for me, it wasn't his shot, but mine. "Good break, Bones," he said. "Now let's see what you can do with it."

I smiled, but I didn't reply. I looked the table over good, silently. I figured my best odds and chose the high balls because most of them were already near a pocket. I worked out an elaborate strategy, including a bridge shot, but I finally decided to just go ahead and shoot. If I pondered any longer, Mose Baker would prod me and make me more nervous than I was already.

I sank six in a row. Then I scratched and missed just when I had Mose sweating for the very first time. It was an easy shot and I still can't believe I missed it. (A flaw in the felt must've curved the ball.) It was the sheriff's fault, partly. He shook the floor as he came storming into the pool room suddenly, but Mose insisted I had already scratched a moment before.

"Is Big Shack in here?" the sheriff asked impatiently, maybe trying to cover up his own nervousness.

If Zeke had looked carefully, he wouldn't have had to ask the question. Big Shack was spitting distance away, and his size made him hard to miss even though his big round evil face was hidden in the shadow of the hooded lamp hanging low over the table just behind us. His chronic asthma gave him the sound of a grizzly bear drawing breath. So Big Shack's loud scratchy rattling throat made him easy to find—or avoid—even in dim smoky light.

"Big Shack!" Zeke called when he finally recognized the huge silhouette.

Slowly, Big Shack dodged his large round brown

head from behind the hanging hooded lamp. He had taken his own sweet time answering. He shot a cold evil stare dead into the sheriff's nervous eyes and replied, "Yeah?"

"Come with me!" the sheriff said, trying to make himself sound tough. But his voice trembled some. Zeke was probably recalling when he and Big Shack had tussled during the strikers' trouble at the Lumber Mill.

"What's up?"

Everything in the pool room had stopped dead still. Every eye was on Big Shack. Would it happen again? was the question scribbled on everybody's face. Seconds ticked away slowly. Zeke didn't know what to expect either. His nervous hand moved closer to his pistol.

The air was thick enough to cut with a knife. After what appeared to be an eternity, Big Shack laid down the cue ball he had been nearly crushing and rolled it hard across the table. It exploded in the opposite corner pocket. Big Shack set his pool stick up in the rack without looking back, with his eyes glued on the sheriff. Then, slowly, he marched past Zeke. The sheriff craned around, tracking him, and only after Big Shack had walked peacefully out the door and stood himself beside the patrol car, looking as tame as a cornered wildcat, did Zeke follow him. And everybody in the pool room followed Zeke outside.

Stiff, tense, and real slow, obviously looking for an unexpected sudden desperate move, the sheriff bent his own bulk to open the rear door for Big Shack. Except for his loud breathing, Big Shack slid into the backseat calmly. Then Zeke closed the door quickly and locked it.

Big Shack resembled a caged grizzly bear stuffed inside the sheriff's car. Not one gawking soul said a word until Zeke's car had cruised slowly down Riverside Lane, with red lights flashing, and cut right sharply up Confederate Drive to go toward Main Street.

"Let's just say you won that one, Bones!" Mose Baker said, breaking the silence. "And we'll call it a day for now."

I couldn't figure out why Mose was in such a hurry to leave. The crowd was getting bigger by the minute. The barbershop had emptied—all the customers had come out to join us—and people were coming like hungry ants. Everyone was excited that the bank robber had finally been caught. Everybody was surprised it was Big Shack, especially since only yesterday I had found the robber's mask in Skip's garbage can. Even though Big Shack was black, he sure didn't fit Betsy's description, but most sensible people had by now discounted that anyway.

In a couple of minutes a cashier from the Piggly Wiggly came out to join the crowd and put everybody straight. Big Shack, who was out of work because he hadn't been rehired when the mill strike ended, had been arrested for shoplifting.

The Piggly Wiggly and almost every other store in town had filed complaints. The sheriff had come to the pool room straight from the Shack place, where he had found enough new clothes to stock a clothing shop, and under the Piggly Wiggly label alone he had found nearly a year's supply of groceries tucked away. Now that he had nabbed Big Shack, Zeke was looking for Tommy, who two salesmen said always tried on three pairs of pants but only brought two back out of the fitting room. I was just dying to tell Bird.

Since in his own clumsy way Fish had tried to defend me, I felt indebted to him, so I invited him to my house to lunch, on the spur of the moment. I invited Mose to come along too, but he said he had something to do. I took it he liked the idea I'd somehow become Fish's close buddy again and he wanted to let us do this alone. Maybe he didn't trust my leaky boat going that far. Smiling, he gave me a teasing whack on my back, like a big brother and quietly told Fish, who was whistling as usual, to stop. I also noted Mose was edging us out of the crowd, and toward my boat.

He accompanied us in the boat as far as their backyard. He offered to row, so I let him. When we reached the far edge of their backyard, by their garden where the bank is best to land, and just as he was about to hand me the oars and say good-bye, Mose Baker angrily said, "Fish, stop that stupid whistling! I keep telling you time and time again, it makes people think you're crazy. Stop it! Right now!"

After I took my oars from him, he stepped out to the bank, walked up toward the garden and stopped, like he regretted that he had yelled at Fish.

205

I was a little surprised Fish's whistling had made him react so sharply. A minute earlier Mose had patted Fish on the back, and in a low, tender voice asked him to stop. Something had gotten Mose Baker upset. He was looking down at a little bald patch in their garden. It was already the middle of August and still no seeds had sprouted. The rest of the garden was up and growing fast. They'd soon have some big tomatoes. Maybe that little patch had been planted just recently, I thought, probably added to Madame Baker's already tall sprouts by Mose after he came home. When he saw I was watching him, he reluctantly turned away.

Trying to lighten things up a bit, I said, "Now you're going to come with me, Mr. Fish."

Flashing his sad watery smile, Fish said, "Um going to go with you, Mr. Bones."

"You be sure to watch your manners, Fish," Mose said, facing us again now, with a tight smile.

"Okay, Sarge," Fish said. "Fish will watch his manners."

"And you don't go around choking anybody else, you hear, Bones?"

"Yes, Sarge!" I said, snapping him a salute he seemed to enjoy. Then, poling slowly, I turned a last time as I began to paddle away from the bank, and saw a strange look in Mose Baker's eyes. Before turning back to the river and setting the oars in to row, I added, "See you later."

"See ya later," Fish echoed me, but Mose only waved.

In the hot sun it feels like an awful long row, but all my sweating wasn't from the heat. I was a bit wary about bringing Fish home with me: I hadn't warned my mother.

We strolled up our back walk toward the porch steps, where Grandma was the first one to see us. She immediately halted her quilting. "Just where do you think you're going?" Grandma asked, staring directly at Fish. I knew her mind was on Fish's past deeds, most of which he was not even responsible for. Grandma wasn't bothering to give him the benefit of the doubt.

I hesitated, to swallow the tension. "To lunch," I pushed out.

"And him?" Grandma asked. Her eyes never left Fish.

I was frozen by Grandma's tone of voice until by some miracle my mother came to the screen door and rescued us from Grandma's stone-paralyzing stare. Searching for just the right words, pretending she was glad to see Fish, my mother said, "Well, look who's here!" Then she rolled her eyes hard at Grandma, and her powerful stare penetrated the steel wire mesh of our screen door and neutralized Grandma's effect upon me. Mother swung open the screen door and quickly I pushed Fish through past Grandma's rocker.

Of course Fish thought it was a game. Once inside our living room he pushed me back, a little too strong, and I almost fell. My mother gave me a look and pointed us toward the bathroom. I knew my folks thought that Fish was weird because he was always wandering about whistling, sometimes humming to himself and doing other people's work for them for free, and even stealing, though not for himself, and more often than not, causing trouble. But he had never done anything to any of us. I thought they were being just a little bit hypocritical, especially since Madame Baker was hairdresser for Bird, Grandma, and my mother.

When Fish and I sat down for lunch, Grandma refused to come to the table. I didn't hold it much against her. She does the same to a lot of company we have. Bird stirred her food around on her plate, too mad to eat. That was easy to figure out, since I'd discovered her and Tommy Shack together behind that mound of garbage. Surely she had already told Mother a bunch of fibs on me behind my back to cover herself. I began to wonder what I'd have to watch out for.

Until my father shut him up, Ford started recalling, out loud, some of the details of Fish's past mishaps. My mother ate very little, but she gave Fish and me two servings with a polite smile.

As I wiped my mouth off, with my napkin this time instead of my sleeve (and motioned for Fish to do the same), I stared hard at Bird across the table. I just knew it would bring her out.

"What you got to stare at, boy?" she whispered at me.

"I guess you heard about Tommy Shack," I said coolly. "Just a while ago he got arrested for stealing enough new clothes to start a clothing store." Surely he must be in custody by now, I thought. I wouldn't have Tommy Shack to worry about anymore.

"You're lying, as usual!" Bird shouted at me. "It's about all you know how to do. I was with him just this mornin'. . . ." Too late, she clapped a hand over her big mouth.

Nobody was disappointed when we left.

CHAPTER SEVENTEEN

I got invited to the Bakers'

J UST LIKE TOAD MAN, Fish had to constantly be told to bail out water. The water was gushing up through the hole in the floor more and more every day. I knew I was going to have to fix it soon. One day I could actually sink. We got back downriver and I was angling us over to the bank behind Fish's house when I saw Mose Baker in the garden fussing over that bald patch of turned earth at the edge of Madame Baker's already tall sprouts. Mose didn't hear us approaching. I started to hail him, then decided to wait until we got closer. I was curious to know what he had planted. I'd seen him in that very same corner yesterday when my father and I had come by to pick up their garbage. He sure seems to be wasting his time adding plants this late in August, I thought. I couldn't see Mose Baker as a gardener anyway.

Suddenly Fish shouted out to him, "Hey Sarge, it's us. Look! Hey, Sarge? Fish!"

Yesterday he had waved to me, but from the look on his face now, Mose Baker wasn't expecting us back so soon. He looked more startled than surprised. Dressed in his Marines uniform, even with the hoe, Mose Baker still looked more like a guard than a gardener. He had caught me observing him. I hoped he hadn't guessed what I'd been thinking.

Fish was up the bank before me because I had to tie up my boat. But I did see Mose Baker grab him and whisper something in his ear. Fish could hardly let him get finished before he began to mouth to me, "Sarge 'n' me invite you to lunch d'morrow, Bones."

All the way home I kept thinking, What's he got planted down there that's precious enough to fuss over in this hot sun, yet never comes up?

Early the next morning before I could slip away, my mother grabbed me. So I had to do some shopping for her first. As I rowed by, I didn't see anybody up the bank at the Bakers', but I did notice the little patch of bald garden looked freshly watered.

Down the plank at the barbershop's landing I tied up next to a few other boats, ran quickly up the saggy boards, and flew past the early checker players out in front of the pool room. Inside the Piggly Wiggly I hurried with my shopping and dodged anybody who'd recognize me so I wouldn't have to talk. Doris' check-out line was somehow always the shortest, so I took

211

advantage, pushing my cart up behind her only customer.

"Howdy, Bones," Doris saluted me even before she was done totaling up the lady in front of me. Doris had acquired a good style. She didn't have to look directly at the cash register to punch the numbers up anymore. When I didn't reply right away she asked, "Everything okay?"

"Yup!" I snapped. "Why shouldn't it be?"

To the lady in front of me, Doris said in a hurry, "That'll be thirty-six ten, please. Here's your receipt, and have a good day!"

I saw from the lady's look she thought Doris' manner was a little pushy. The lady plunked four crinkled bills and a dime down into Doris' waiting palm, snatched her package from the bag boy, and strode out of the Piggly Wiggly without replying to Doris' "have a good day." Not bothered at all, Doris placed the bills into the right compartments and dropped the ten-cent piece into a pool of dimes without once looking down.

I was impressed, but I was in a hurry too. "Move up," she said to me to sound important.

I pushed my cart up and put my purchases onto the moving belt. Doris rang them up, then reached over and tenderly caressed my hand.

The impatient customer behind me grunted.

"Sixteen forty, Bones!" Doris said, after she hit the total button with her thumb. Doris went into her cash drawer, quickly gave me three sixty change, pressing the coins heavily into my palm atop the bills, and let her soft thumb linger there as she smiled over to me. "Receipt's with your change, Bones, and have a good day."

I really do like Doris more than I show her, though sometimes I find her just a mite too pushy. I took my sack from the bag boy and loped away, ducking out of the Piggly Wiggly in a hurry to take the shortcut through Dish Water Alley. In my haste, where the alley ends on this side of the railroad tracks, I bumped into my father and Toad Man casually collecting the endless pile of the Piggly Wiggly's garbage.

"Howdy, Bones, long time no see!" Toad Man said. "What's your hurry?"

You devil, I thought. After what you did to me, a long time is too short. I said, "Hello." Raising the bag of groceries up over my chest, I squeezed around the garbage truck as fast as I could push through the tight little space they had left against the wall. "I've got some frozen stuff in here. I've got to get it home in a hurry." And I took off across the tracks.

As I rowed upriver, about even with Riverside Flats, which sat along the bank at the south end of the Bottom, I saw a crowd milling about at the front entrance. I eased over to the bank, tied up, and went to see what all the fuss was about so early.

The notorious housing project, where most of Duck Tanner's bunch lived, was purposely built high to protect it from flooding when the Bottom filled up with water every spring. I saw Duck Tanner standing in front of the crowd. All of his cronies were with him

213

except Short Billy. Today was Friday, and payday; still for some reason they were all late for work. All these people couldn't be waiting for Short Billy, I thought. Then I saw everyone was looking up toward Short Billy's room on the second floor. After I saw Zeke's car, I didn't need to ask what was going on.

Through his window, I could see Short Billy holding up what appeared to be a paper airplane and nervously weaving it through the air while explaining something to the sheriff, who was holding what was obviously some paper money.

"Now, who could've set up our little Billy?" Duck Tanner was asking for the third time since I had been standing there, while shifting his cap and looking around to appraise the crowd. "This is exactly the same thing that happened to y'all, fellows." Duck looked around speaking to Nat Tripper, Barny Clay, and Jim Bowles, who had been arrested this same day three weeks ago.

"Not exactly the same way, Duck," Nat corrected Duck, stuttering. "The m-m-money was p-p-planted in our p-p-pockets on a clothesline. But it s-s-sure was s-s-somebody with a good aim to throw a p-p-paper airplane up that high and not m-m-miss Short Billy's w-w-window."

"And imagine, carrying a fifty-dollar bill!" Jim Bowles added.

"A bad one!" Barny Clay added his bit, shaking his head.

"Hee, hee, hee," Charley Price, the last of Duck Tanner's cronies, the comedian of the bunch, laughed, and said, "And he only gave—er, planted—on y'all a ten-spot. Seems he thought Short Billy was worth more!"

"This ain't no laughing matter, Chick!" Duck turned around again, using Charley's nickname, showing everybody who was the boss. "Boys, we figure out who did this to our little Billy, and we got ourselves a bank robber and a thousand-dollar reward," he added, scratching his big wide nose, acting as if he was the king of the Bottom, like an old gangster, though he'd only recently dropped out of high school along with the rest of them.

No matter what they wanted to believe (he was their buddy), Short Billy was nothing but a thug. He gambled with Duck and the rest every single day and almost always lost, piling up a string of gambling debts that he somehow always found enough money to pay. This made him a number-one candidate in my book. If it had been anybody else, I would've felt a little sorry for him. Short Billy, never.

The growing cold, wet spot on my chest reminded me of my mother's frozen stuff I was holding. (I hadn't left them inside the boat for fear someone from Riverside Flats might steal them.) I had to get them home in a hurry before they melted, or my mother would kill me.

When I got back to town after dropping off the groceries, Long Mose Baker and Fish were waiting for me along the bank behind their lot. I tied my bow rope to a few blades of long grass. I was in such a hurry, I left half the boat in the water. "Y'all heard about Short Billy, I reckon?" I asked, anxious to know what had happened since I left.

Mose Baker had the squint on his face I noticed he wore when he was thinking. He hung one arm around Fish's shoulder. "The sheriff did nothing but warn him about his drinking and tell him not to leave town all of a sudden," he said, sounding personally disappointed. Eighteen was quite young to be a heavy drinker, I thought. "He had a good alibi for everything except his smell," Mose Baker added, like he was talking about someone he really hated. Maybe he had somehow found out that it was Short Billy who'd issued Fish the dare that day at the ball field.

"Some stinking alibi!" Fish said, like he was repeating something he had just overheard.

"That means he wasn't the bank robber either?" I said. Then I wondered out loud, "Who could've thrown that paper airplane up there through the window to his room and then just vanished like that?"

"You can think much better on a full stomach," Mose Baker said.

As we climbed up the bank, I glanced over toward the garden. I didn't get a real good look because I felt Mose watching me, which was strange, considering it was just a lousy garden. I was sure I saw nothing growing over there in that corner where he'd been fussing around.

We ducked into their house through the back door and surprised Madame Baker in her kitchen beauty

216

parlor. The counter was messy with beauty chemicals. Bottles of hair dye were strewn about nearly everywhere. I saw a thawing package of hamburger meat near some hair dye, and I immediately got butterflies in my stomach.

We had disturbed Madame Baker while she was busy cleaning up the morning's clippings of hair. "You should really go into the wig business, Momma," Mose Baker said, teasing her.

"Sarge, I've told you a thousand times not to bring company inside my beauty parlor until after twelve o'clock, when it becomes a kitchen again!" Madame Baker seemed more embarrassed than angry, and when she straightened up with her dustpan full of hair, I saw once more where Mose got his tallness from. They were almost the same height, though where he had muscles, she had a flabbiness. Madame Baker had a lot of wrinkles for a lady her age, and although she smiled, there was an anger, or a sadness, under the surface of her dark face, similar to Mose's bitter expression and quite different from Fish's faraway, empty look.

"Oh, Bones isn't company, Momma." Mose Baker slapped my back.

"All menfolks're company in a woman's beauty parlor," Madame Baker said. "Now get out o' here 'til I call you!"

We dodged quickly across the kitchen and out of range of Madame Baker's broom. Fish and I followed Mose down a long, dark hallway to their living room. Mose pointed me to the sofa. Fish slipped down beside

217

me while Mose went over to a musty wooden cabinet and pulled out a picture album. Sitting atop the cabinet, somewhat in shadow (actually the whole house seemed dark and foreboding), was a fading picture that had to be Mose Baker's father. Mose resembled him. Fish, not at all. Mose caught me having a quick look around.

"My service pictures," Mose Baker said, opening the thick, padded, olive-green book. Then pointing out his Marine buddies, he started to tell me a joke with every picture he showed me. Seeing Mose Baker laughing, with his arms around all those Marine pals of his, was strange. Under one picture, one with a white soldier, were scribbled the words, "Thank you buddy, for crawling through the mud under a hail of Cong bullets to pull me out." Signed, "Little Gilly, from Macon, Georgia, Sept. 1969, Saigon, in the Nam." I had never before thought of Mose Baker as a person who had friends. He sure never had any around town. To me, he seemed to be one of those people who changed moods quickly, and had two sides to him, if not more. Looking at the various Mose Bakers, I wondered why he had chosen me to buddy up with. I badly wanted to ask him, but he was so moody I was afraid my curiosity would rub him the wrong way. I really wanted to know a little more about his father, too. I saw another picture of him up on the mantel above their fake fireplace. "Look at this one," Mose said, pointing back at the album, when he saw me looking around again.

"Look at this one," Fish echoed him.

Mose Baker was firing a machine gun with the same bitter squint I had seen so often on his face. There was another picture of him holding a heavy bazooka, loaded and ready to fire. He hit his chest with a fist when he pointed to his first parachute jump. The jump plane was flying off in a cloudy background. There was also one of him half inside of a combat-ready tank, in camouflage. In the last one he showed me, Mose Baker was standing on the wings of a jet. "I'm no pilot, though," he said. "That's for the real brains. I'm combat!"

Seeing the one with the jet reminded me of Short Billy's paper airplane. I was thinking, Ummmmm, when I heard footsteps in the hall. Madame Baker stuck her bushy head into the living room, poking it through the curtain of long stringy beads that served as a room divider and a fly blocker. For a hairdresser she had the worst-looking head of hair of anybody in Sun City. "Hamburgers are ready," she said.

"You mean hairburgers!" Mose Baker said, teasing her.

"Hairburgers!" Fish parroted him.

I didn't find it funny. Mose Baker and Fish sat down eager to eat. While Madame Baker poured hefty glasses of Coke around the table, I eased down, taking a good look about. The stove was clear. But the counter was still littered with beauty parlor accessories. I carried my hamburger up toward my mouth, taking my time. I bit real hesitantly, in small bites, but I kept imagining that the juices dripping out of my burger were the same as the stuff I saw coming down the sides of the jars scattered upon the counter. A reddish fluid was leaking out of an overturned bottle near the chopping board. The board was still stained where the madame had pounded out her patties. The colors matched. I began to chew slower, the beauty parlor fumes bringing a mist to my eyes, same as when I peel onions. The odor of damp hair drifted up my nose and down my windpipe. I felt a cough coming on. The taste of my burger reminded me of my mother's hairdo.

"You want another one, Bones?" Madame Baker asked, waving a fork at me, ready to get up even before I answered.

"Ah, I'm not done with this one yet," I replied, and began to nibble slower on my burger to make it last. Looking around and hoping I wasn't so obvious this time, I started thinking about Mose Baker's story, trying to picture that night the Klan took his father away and lynched him. In which room had the struggle taken place? In this kitchen, maybe? What time of night was it? Just how many were there, exactly? Who really were those "others" Mose had mentioned? Mose Baker had also said his father had shouted for Madame Baker to bring a pistol. Why hadn't he had it ready? Hadn't he suspected that they were coming to get him? Why hadn't he given some sort of warning, told some other black men, friends, to be on the lookout? Didn't at least one of the neighbors hear any strange noises that night—Madame Baker screaming for help, two-year-old Mose crying more than usual in the middle of night? Was it the same pistol Fish had shot himself in the head with seven years ago, in this very kitchen, I wondered, twelve years after that much worse event? I looked down at my empty hands and realized I'd somehow finished eating my burger. I sure didn't have the stomach to eat another one now.

"Care for some dessert?" Madame Baker asked.

"No thanks," I said. "I'm full." I had to wiggle out of the madame's dessert with that polite lie, even though I do like strawberries inside Jell-O. Just now they reminded me of her hair dye, and other things, like blood. Hoping my face didn't expose my fib, forcing a smile, and already feeling a bad case of gas coming on, I said I had really enjoyed myself.

"Enough for a couple of games of pool?" Mose Baker asked.

"Er, yeah," I said, eager to get out of Madame Baker's kitchen. I was the first up. I wiped my mouth on my sleeve fast, threw Fish a fake punch to his full round stomach, and beat them to the back door. I opened the screen, bounced down the steps, and tried to force a burp as I walked on ahead, sneaking a peep at Mose Baker's little bald garden on my way to the river trail.

"What's the big hurry?" Mose called from far behind me.

"What's the big hurry?" Fish echoed him.

"I'm in a hurry to beat you," I said back over my shoulder. "And this time I'm not going to make it easy."

Except for Big Shack, who was in jail, the usual crowd was in the pool room (I wondered now how Big

221

Shack ever took all the smoke with his asthma). I was choosing my stick off the rack when Mose, rubbing his hands together, walked in with Fish a minute behind me. The burgers seemed to have given him more energy. Mose Baker said, "Wanna try a betting game now?"

I had indigestion, but I couldn't tell him that. I said, "You must be kidding. I'm flat broke."

"Your credit's good," Mose Baker said, racking up the balls before going to choose his own stick.

I whacked the cue ball sharply. I struck it at a perfect angle and sent the balls scattering. It was a good spread. I chose the high balls immediately for their ideal positions. Three sat almost inside pockets.

"You sure learned how to break!" Mose said.

I just smiled. Then I sank my first ball with a clean kiss that left the cue ball where it struck.

"Good shooting!" Mose Baker said.

I sank seven in a row. I scratched on the eight ball. "Shucks! That's where I always screw up."

"Then look a little closer at this," Mose Baker said, and quickly he cleared everything off the table except the eight ball in one unbroken run. He rechalked his cue stick to make sure he wouldn't scratch, then he took a long, slow aim.

Just before he made the shot, I threw him a question. "What in the world do you have planted out there in that bald-headed little patch at the corner of your garden that's never come up?"

I can't swear I saw him tremble, though he blinked

and scratched his shot, missing the eight ball, wide. He did push out a quick answer. "Just some seeds I got from the Piggly Wiggly."

"Nothing's ever come up?" I asked again.

After an overly long pause, he replied dryly, "Not yet."

CHAPTER EIGHTEEN

On a hunch I decided
to risk a visit to
Mad Doc Holden

MOSE BAKER WON THE GAME, but it took him longer than ever before. Maybe he was just fooling around to tease me, although I don't think so because of the look on his face. We played a couple more games. They really weren't the same as all the others. When I left him and Fish up the landing around three and walked down the plank, I still felt his eyes on me. Stepping inside my boat, I turned, waved and said I was going home. I wasn't.

Because Mose Baker might have been watching, instead of going the shortest way, I rowed upriver and took a roundabout route to the Gilmore Plantation. I wasn't sure it was a wise move to go disturb Mad Doc Holden, though he was the one person who could give me the proof I needed to be sure that what I was think-

224

ing now I was not just imagining. Anyone in town will tell you Doc Holden is a raving-mad lunatic, and not only because he chose to live on the wrong side of the river in a place haunted by the ghosts of a thousand slaves. I shoved aside my fear and squeezed my boat through a stand of high reeds, tying up as close to the bank as I could get. I hopped out in shallow water on a mud bar, getting my shoes wet, and I crept up the bank and fought my way through tall weeds until I reached the disappearing old road leading up to the rotting main house of the spooky Gilmore Plantation where Doc squats illegally.

The bridge that comes over the river was condemned long ago when it got too shaky to cross, and Mad Doc Holden and the Shacks got cut off on this side without a safe way to get to town. Mad Doc Holden put some boards together and made himself a raft. It's not that sturdy, so he only uses it at low water, when it hasn't rained for a while. Even then, rarely. The crazy Shacks are foolish enough to still use the bridge, which could fall down at any moment. They take a real big chance on foot every day. I feel I'm taking a big bold risk every time I paddle under the badly bowing trestle, but there is no other way to get downriver by boat. So I always look up and cross my heart first, praying the Shacks' old bridge doesn't collapse while I'm under it. My father made the Shacks agree to a deal a long while back to bring their garbage across the bridge to the town side. That's where he and Toad Man pick it up. Mad Doc Holden chucks his few throw-outs into his front yard. Some he pitches straight into the river.

I walked cautiously, looking about for a tall, dark, wild-looking figure in an old faded baseball uniform, probably carrying a loaded double-barreled shotgun instead of a bat. Mad Doc Holden had dreamed all of his life about being a famous strike-out pitcher in the major leagues. Doc's favorite team was the New York Yankees, although he had said once he would even play for the Atlanta Braves if they drafted him. I knew Doc had written many a misspelled letter to various big-league scouts. He once even paid his own fare over to Tallahassee—although it doesn't even have a minor-league team—just for the chance to pitch a free exhibition game for the state college scouts. Doc hoped he would be discovered before they found out he didn't finish high school. He hoped they'd like his stuff enough not to let him go.

It rained the whole week Doc was in Tallahassee waiting. He ran out of money and his hotel kicked him out. He got roughed up by a policeman who caught him sleeping in the Greyhound bus terminal. The policeman roused Doc awake, frisked him, and found a return ticket to Sun City in his pocket. The policeman put Doc on the first bus heading west. Doc never even saw a pitcher's mound.

Six years ago a scout for the Atlanta Braves did answer one of Doc's badly written letters. It read, "If you can pitch better than you can spell, then do pay us a visit here in Atlanta. We'd love to see your 'stuff.' We

226

don't have any scouts hounding the Sun City area at the present. And I'm sorry, but our policy won't allow us to advance you a ticket before we've seen just what you can do." The letter was signed, "Don 'Home-Run' Reed, Former All-Star Slugger and Chief Look-Out for the famed Atlanta Braves."

Doc showed the letter every day to just about everybody in town while he worked at the lumber mill to save up his fare. He carried it around inside his sweaty pocket until it fell apart. Doc had taped it up and it was still in one jagged piece a year later when he paraded it around town one last time to announce he had the fare to Atlanta. It was just before Doc was to take off for Atlanta that he was the star pitcher in the doubleheader for our local Sun City sandlot team. The series had been specially sponsored to celebrate Doc's big send-off.

That was the day Fish Baker stuck his face through the jagged hole ripped into the chicken-wire backstop screen behind the catcher and Doc Holden's famous fast curvy spitball found it poking through the rip—a stone-hard baseball straight to Fish's temple—five long years ago, and Doc has punished himself ever since. That day, Doc wept and cursed himself so, I can still vividly remember his tears falling on Fish's still body, the bleachers emptying, a curious crowd swarming around Fish as Madame Baker cupped his swollen head in her lap while Mose Baker knelt, fanning him, and Doc, bellowing like a sow, begging Fish to hang on. Afterward, when news came from the hospital that

227

Fish had changed color and gone into a deep coma, Doc began to drink heavily, raging about town in a drunken stupor and labeling himself a child crippler. The stress cracked Doc up. He took to the woods, which is about all that's left of the old Gilmore place.

Doc is rarely seen in town anymore, and I saw from the condition of the road that Doc didn't get many visitors. About once every six months he shows up on his raft, then vanishes again like a ghost after buying a half-year's supply of dog food, but little else. He's never come to town with a dog, so I wasn't worried about that. I was jumpy because I once saw Doc brandishing a shotgun along the river's edge. It seemed silly to be guarding some unwanted run-down property from trespassers until I saw the duck floating along the river. Doc aimed and missed, standing right on top of it, so like the duck, I knew I needed to spot him first. I didn't.

"Who're you, yonder?" Mad Doc's voice crackled behind me. "Be quick about it. My aim's not as bad as it's rumored to be. If I do miss, this dog here is very hungry. And he likes stuck-ups."

A dog started a low growl. The scratchy sound raised up gradually to a bone-chilling howl and cut off suddenly. It sounded like the dog had swallowed up his own voice.

"Bonapart!" I answered, trembling. "My father used to collect your garbage before Shack's bridge got too risky to cross." He really couldn't label me a "stuck-up."

228

"You just turn around real slowly," Doc ordered.

I craned around, almost squeaking from fear. Doc appraised my face. His big dog eyed me like a meal. "You're who you say you are, all right," Doc croaked after a long squint, "and I ought to let my hungry dog chase after you like your grandpa's old bull Satan once charged me when I took a shortcut across his pasture."

I felt lucky he recognized me. Him bringing up something very unpleasant that had happened to him many years ago told me his memory was good too. His threat frightened the sweat out of me, though.

Slowly, I saw his eyes change. He seemed amused by my shaking. "Don't worry, Bones. I've got some human feelings left in me yet, and I ain't as crazy as most people think. Now tell me just what brought you across a bridge most intelligent folks won't go near."

"I came by boat," I said.

"A real smart thing to do," Doc said. "Still, what brings you over here?"

"I came to see you, Mr. Holden," I said trembling, with my hands still high in the air like I was surrendering.

"You can drop your spidery hands now," Doc said. "They make me nervous. And ain't nothing out here worth stealing."

I lowered my hands. Doc scratched his long scraggly beard and narrowed his wild bloodshot eyes down to a slit. For someone who was just twenty-seven years old, he resembled an unkempt grandfather more than a failed black baseball pitcher. Doc hadn't cut his hair for a very long time, so he could've been taken for a mad professor in a baseball cap, too. He obviously wasn't eating enough. His dark pockmarked face had sunk so close to the bones, I could almost see his skull. Doc was skinny as a nail, and his lankiness reminded me of Mose Baker some, except that Doc had no muscles. I could count his ribs through a rip in his dingy faded baseball uniform, and his smell reminded me of Toad Man.

For a moment it appeared he was having a drunk's quick blackout on his feet. Not sure if I should chance a quick move, I looked down the barrel of the unsteady shotgun he still had pointed at me—him half asleep. I had changed my mind. I wanted to leave. It had been a big mistake to disturb him. Then suddenly, his wild dark eyes opened back up from the squint and pored over me like he was surprised I was standing there. "Er, where was we?" he asked.

"I was about to tell you why I came out here," I said, shakily.

"Go on."

I said, "There are a lot of strange things happening around town lately. Maybe you've heard about some of them."

"Strange things?" Doc said.

I didn't really know how to say what I'd come to say. I found myself thinking, The bank got robbed—you must know. (Maybe he knew. Maybe he didn't.) You must know that, even though the robber hasn't been caught yet, bits of the bank's money have popped back up quite mysteriously. Not by any means accidentally, I'm sure. Because the embarrassing trick hasn't been played on everybody in town, just certain individuals. If the bank robber had been a stranger, he would've had to have quit town right away, in a big hurry. Otherwise, he would look real suspicious, and would already have been caught. Whoever it was who robbed the Bank of Sun City hasn't left town at all, I wanted to say. It must be somebody everybody knows, somebody who's sure he'll never be suspected and somebody with a good reputation. No one has turned up missing. Nobody has left town suddenly, and anybody who does leave town for a day or two comes back right away and has a spotless reason for having left in the first place. One person died. She wasn't the bank robber, although she almost got buried with a fifty-dollar bill in her casket that was traced back to the bank robbery.

How could I say all this to Doc? If I did, I'd have to end up with something real touchy—the very reason behind his madness. He saw I was unsure by the way I was scratching my head.

"I guess you're not a drinking man?" Doc asked, pulling a bottle out of his pocket and twisting the cork off with a pop.

Even though I had inched back some without him noticing, just the little whiff I got from his bottle of smelly old whiskey was strong enough to make me blink like I had sniffed camphor. "Er, not yet."

"Too bad. This stuff has a way of opening a scared fellow up." He took a long swallow. It was apparently so bitter that even he frowned, his eyes closed. I watched a leak trickle down his chin and run to his Adam's apple before zigzagging down inside his dingy shirt. Since his eyes were closed, and he held the bottle up so long, I figured maybe he had fallen asleep. I took the opportunity to observe him closer and discovered he was just squinting, observing me through the glass.

I knew I had to think up something quick before he lost his patience with me or his whiskey turned him sour. Suddenly, a way occurred to me how I could get out of Doc what I wanted without upsetting him. I couldn't risk mentioning Fish Baker's name, nor could I go and tell him I'd come to see him about a bank robbery. I couldn't tell him that all the suspects on the sheriff's long list had one thing in common with him: Either they had made the foolish mistake of mistreating Fish Baker, as was the case with all the black people under suspicion, or they were somehow (I was sure) connected directly or indirectly to the lynching of Mose Baker's father in the swamp, as was the case with most of the white people under suspicion.

I thought, This thing really started a long time ago, way back when Mose Baker was younger, though it was the trick he played with the snake at the rodeo and that snake planted in the Bar & Grill that first made me suspect him.

Doc's name had to be high on Mose Baker's list of people to get even with, because it was Doc's fastball that had put Fish in a coma. Though really Short Billy was more to blame. In my opinion, Skip was number

232

one, because he had sent Fish into Abernathy's Swamp for that alligator, Skip who had sent Fish parading around town with old lady Riley's bloomers on a pole like they were a flag, and also Skip who had told Fish to go after undertaker T. L. Hooker's goldfish. That's why Skip got that stack of bills planted in his car at his wedding, I suspect, and later the pig mask planted in the Bar & Grill's garbage can. Mr. Pete was obvious because, if not the leader, he had been a member of the Klan party that had lynched Mose Baker's father. That's why that poisonous snake was planted inside the Bar & Grill, and it almost bit Betsy instead. Though the trick at the wedding and the mask in the garbage can appeared to have been aimed at Skip, it's probably more accurate to say that both were done to get back at Mr. Pete as well.

I believe now the water in Mrs. Crawley's birdbath was poisoned, as she had always insisted. I'm also quite sure now Mr. Smarty, Mr. Baxter's cat, was killed, too. After seeing Mose Baker shoot that bullfrog in the swamp, I knew he was capable of doing both these things. Both Mrs. Crawley's husband and Mr. Baxter had always been two of Mr. Pete's best friends.

Four years ago someone poured a pound of sugar into the gas tank of Mr. Bullers' Mack truck and destroyed the motor. Mr. Bullers was a very good friend of Mr. Pete's, too. They were almost inseparable, as I'd just seen again Tuesday night in the skating rink.

I remembered some talk I'd heard about a black man who had tried to unionize Sun City's lumber mill,

233

back twenty years ago, long before the recent strike. Could that black man have been Mose Baker's father? The lumber mill belonged to Mr. Cutter, who owned the Bank of Sun City, too. Mr. Cutter was a very close friend of Mr. Pete's also, so I could imagine they could have been together the night Mose Baker's father was dragged away. Being the richest man in town, Mr. Cutter was used to giving orders. Could he have been a leader in the Klan nineteen years ago? Was that why his bank had been robbed?

All the white people who'd had things done to them over the years that were still unexplained might have good reason to suspect a Baker, but not Fish, although he'd taken the blame for a lot of things; and all the black people too might just as well suspect Mose Baker—like Short Billy, who'd issued that dare five years ago, and had just received a fifty via a paper airplane. Short Billy had almost gotten arrested, but Nat Tripper, Jim Bowles, and Barny Clay had not been so lucky three weeks earlier.

All four—Short Billy, Nat, Barny, and Jim—were members of Duck Tanner's gang, and Mose Baker had a good reason to hate every last one of them. Though I think the trick played on the undertaker—the money planted in old lady Riley's casket and on Reverend Black's clothesline—was just to muddle things (although, Reverend Black had always used Fish to mow his lawn for free).

Dropping his snake at the rodeo was Mose Baker's

234

way of getting back at the whole town. The big trick started with the bank robbery. Then, right afterward, those misleading plants, first on three black people, then on a white person. This clever switchup caused so much confusion that everybody, black and white alike, even the people who should've been able to see through the trick, especially those with one particular thing in common—Fish Baker—were blinded by it. Neither they nor the sheriff could see because Mose Baker had been smart enough to twist things up in such a knot, even to the point of looking clumsy. It worked, while he looked innocent in his Marines uniform.

Looking up at Doc now, so nervous I could hardly believe what I was thinking was possible—though nothing else made any sense—I still couldn't say to him that people were being accused of robbing the Bank of Sun City because someone nobody saw and nobody suspected got close enough to them to plant damaging evidence. But if Doc had received any unexpected money, I'd be closer to proving my theory. "You haven't by any chance received any unexpected mail, have you, Mr. Holden?" I asked.

Doc looked at me real quizzically before he replied. I could see he thought I was crazy. His eyes narrowed to an untrusting slit again, and he reached a hand down to pat his big dog. "Just why would I?" he asked. "I don't even have a mailbox—Aha! You're working for the post office. I finally got a letter from a baseball scout!"

I hadn't thought of that before, and I had to get off that track fast. I shook my head and tried another angle. "You found any strange paper inside your pants pockets after you took them off the clothesline?" I asked.

"I don't have a clothesline neither," Doc replied, squinting at me curiously. "I got only one pair of pants—a baseball uniform, the one I got on."

It should've been obvious to me. I tried once more. "No one has planted anything around here lately, have they?" I asked.

"Just weeds," Doc replied.

"I guess you haven't seen any paper airplanes flying around in the air suspiciously?" I asked.

Doc looked at me oddly. I began to wonder if he'd ever reply.

"I guess you didn't."

I could see he really thought I was the mad one.

"Guess I'll be going now," I said, and suddenly I heard an overburdened groan, a loud *creak! crack!* and a swooshing splash like a big tree had fallen into the river, and not far off.

Doc saw I was startled. "Nothing but the Shacks," he said to reassure me. "Their electricity's been cut off now for a spell, so they chop down trees on my property, sometimes. Those Shacks're mad, so I'd best go have a look. Ain't no need for you to rush off before I get back. I don't get much company over here, even if you didn't bring any mail with you."

His property! Doc *has* gone mad, I thought. I began

to wonder what it really was I'd heard. I said, "I'd best be going, Mr. Holden. I left my boat tied up over there in the reeds, and it takes on water."

Big Shack's locked up in jail, I thought. How could he be chopping down a tree?

CHAPTER NINETEEN

Tommy Shack's revenge

I DROPPED THE OARS DOWN into the river again and gave them a strong pull to correct my drift, letting myself float downriver slowly so I could think. If my suspicions were correct, then why had Mad Doc Holden been left out? Maybe Mose Baker thought Doc had already suffered enough by going mad. Doc really couldn't be held responsible because Fish poked his head through that rip in the backstop screen. Then again, maybe what I'd been thinking was all wrong.

It was around five o'clock now. I was in no hurry to look Mose Baker in his eyes again until I got my head clear. So I barely glanced over to the bank as I coasted up closer to the old sagging oak. When I bumped up against the wobbly mooring at the barbershop landing and did look up the plank, I was expecting to see Fish and Mose Baker beaming down the old shaky plank at me.

They weren't there. Instead, all the regulars were emptying out of the pool room in one great big hurry. My first thought was fire, because only something real serious could budge the regulars from those pool tables. No hint of smoke came from the pool hall. I tied up my boat, hopped to the plank, and raced up to Riverside Lane.

Old man Pool was the slowest to exit. I grabbed him as he tortoised out. "What in the world is going on, Mr. Pool?" I asked, holding on to the sleeve of his tweed suit jacket.

"You mean you haven't heard?"

I said I hadn't. He looked at me as if to ask, And where have you been? while I waited impatiently for a reply. Finally he said, "Word just passed that Shack's old bridge slipped away. That's where I'm heading now!"

So that's the loud crashing sound I heard over at Mad Doc's, I thought, and while I was still thinking, old man Pool snatched his sleeve out of my hand and left me standing there.

I didn't bother to use my boat. I quickly overtook old man Pool and left him far behind as I dashed off downriver toward Shack's bridge.

Mose Baker was standing out front of the big crowd at the edge of the cliff where the bridge had broken away. He was gazing down into the river as if he'd lost something, but nothing was down there except water. The whole bridge had disappeared. Every inch of rotten wood on both sides had collapsed. The decayed stubs once holding up the bridge had got sheared off so smoothly, they looked like they'd been cut with a saw. All the rotten timber had broken up and floated down the river.

Tommy Shack was the only person on the other side. He was dancing about, swearing his innocence, crying a river of tears and wailing like a stuck pig, "I didn't mean to do it!"

I'd thought he was already locked up. Overhearing a few whispers, I began to understand. Although Big Shack was in jail, Tommy hadn't been arrested yet. He'd escaped the sheriff by going over the bridge, knowing Zeke wouldn't eagerly follow him. Zeke's excuse was his hands were so full with the bank robbery, he hadn't the time to go running after a juvenile, putting it off for later. The truth was Zeke was in no hurry for another trip over Shack's old bridge just to pull a frisky handcuffed Tommy back with him, having to test every plank before he stepped on it.

Tommy had picked his way across the dangerous bridge daily for years ever since it was condemned. He knew which planks could be trusted and which ones not to touch. Tommy also knew one good hard blow or a false step would send Shack's bridge crashing down into the river.

The rest of the story made my blood freeze. Tommy had lured Fish Baker across the bridge, probably to get

240

back at him for standing up for me at the dump and the pool room yesterday. I looked at Tommy across the river, him shouting back to the gaping crowd, jumping up and down, looking much like he was a clown on a stage alone, and everyone silently watching him send his dumb stupid apologies over to Mose Baker.

Tommy was lucky Mose Baker couldn't reach him. He was fortunate I couldn't get to him neither.

"I'm donating all my boats!" Old Rufus shouted after he elbowed his way through the crowd to get to the sheriff and Mose Baker. "Good luck." And looking over at me, he added, "But nobody under eighteen is to handle them."

"You can count on my boat too." Skip Goodweather burst through the crowd.

I looked around. Of all people, I never expected this of Skip.

"Time's a-wasting," the sheriff shouted. "Let's get going!"

"I'm coming with you," I said to Mose Baker, looking slightly downward to avoid his eyes, feeling guilty because of what I had been thinking about him earlier.

I seemed to have snapped him out of a trance. Mose didn't say anything; he seemed to be thinking. He sure has got guts, I thought.

Mose Baker handled the tiller and we took the lead. I took the lookout up in the prow. Skip Goodweather led the right wing. The sheriff was on our left. So we had a long chain of boats to drag the river. Everywhere we found a stand of reeds along the bank thick enough to catch anything floating past, we made a closer search. Slowly, we covered every inch of river between the sawed-off bridge and the falls.

I spotted Fish first. "There he is—over there!" I pointed from the prow. Near some rocks, Fish was strangely upright in the rushing water, not far from the spot where Mose Baker had played around with us on Tuesday when he pretended he had lost control of the boat.

I turned to look at Mose.

His eyes held mine for a second. Then he squeezed on the throttle and we lurched suddenly forward. It was all reflex, a desperate attempt to get to Fish, but he was forgetting about the rocks, and the falls were right in front of us. Or was he?

"Stop!" I shouted. "We can't go over there in this thing!" I looked down and saw the rock just as we started over it. I was sure it would tear up through the bow where I sat. I got bounced up suddenly and dropped back down with a sharp jar.

"Get the hell out of there quick, Baker, before it's too late!" the sheriff shouted to us.

A second rock started to rip up through the middle. It tore a gash in front of Mose Baker and the tiller, slicing through the aluminum hull like a can opener. I got launched into the air like a missile and was sure I'd go smashing into a rock.

I landed in clear water and started thrashing, but the swift current held me and was sweeping me directly into the falls. Water was going up my nose. I sucked some in through my mouth, swallowed and started coughing, smelling my own blood. I had to squint tightly, because the cold water rushing into my eyes was chilling me so they burned. Through a slit I saw Mose Baker try to save what was left of the boat so he could go rescue Fish, but he hit one rock, then got hurled into another one that sent him sailing high into the air. Mose Baker went flushing into the fast water shooting up a spray. I saw him drop over the falls and disappear.

I thought the rocks were holding Fish, so I tried to grab hold of one as I washed into him. When my hands slipped over the moldy, glassy surface, I realized if I couldn't anchor myself with something quick, I would get swept past Fish and follow Mose Baker over the falls.

I groped blindly for Fish's legs. After I got hold of one, I braced myself into the rock at Fish's back. It was enough to break my rush over the falls. I pulled against the current until I wedged myself between the two big rocks that held Fish. My right leg washed between Fish's legs, and the current forced it into the gap the water was rushing through.

I was anchored, but unsteadily. I hugged Fish's cold slick body, smelling a strange rot. As his arms collapsed across my shoulders, some blood rushed from somewhere, seeping into my clinging wet shirt, and I discovered it wasn't just the rocks holding Fish there. A plank from Shack's bridge was driven straight through Fish's heart and out the back of his rib cage. It was the plank wedged into the gap where my leg was now stuck that was holding Fish. My bile rose close up to the back of my tongue and sat there, as I shivered and wished myself someplace else.

The swiftly rushing water was slowly sucking my leg farther into the gap. It was Fish who held me back. His gaping frozen eyes stared at me. It looked like Fish wanted to say some last thing to me. But he was already dead, and the cold water was gradually turning him gray.

I couldn't stand to look at him, yet I knew I couldn't close my eyes. I'd never even touched a dead body before, yet we were stuck together now, clutching one another, in a wedge where two swift sweepover currents met; and if I moved either way, or let go of Fish, I would go quickly over the rocks and tumble down the falls. But first, my wedged leg would surely snap.

Tons of icy water poured over us. For an eternity I was aware of just the roaring water and nothing else. I was deliberately looking away from Fish, which was real difficult considering the position I was in. I was desperately trying not to even think. Skip Goodweather must've yelled my name out almost a million times before I finally realized it was me he was calling. *"Bones! Bones! Bones!"*

I couldn't see him because I was facing the falls, and I was afraid to let go of Fish for even a moment to turn and answer. So I nodded my head to let Skip know he had gotten my attention.

"I'm going to throw you a rope," Skip shouted, "and when you get it, just relax and take your time, slowly, because the water is a lot stronger than you are. Are you listening?"

I nodded my head again.

It took three throws before the rope fell at just the right place so it would float to me. Cautiously, I reached out to it, grabbed it, and slowly looped it securely around Fish and me before I attempted to move. It took all the energy I had left to pull my trapped leg out of the gap in the rocks.

I rested and tried to stand up, but the current upset my balance immediately. "Easy, Bones!" Skip called to me.

The sheriff's group threw me another rope and pulled slowly from the opposite bank. The two cross ropes checked my drift toward the falls; Fish's added weight was both a help and a hindrance. We bobbed up and down off the bottom like a cork. My feet kept slipping backward.

Slowly, with Fish in my arms, I was pulled to the bank.

"Good God Almighty!" Skip gasped as he lifted Fish.

I hadn't realized how heavy Fish was until Skip relieved me of his weight. A couple of men from Skip's group helped lower Fish to the ground and cover him up. It wasn't easy with the plank going through his chest.

"How's Mose Baker?" I gasped as someone wrapped me in a blanket.

"We haven't been able to find him yet," the sheriff said.

I collapsed in Skip's arms.

CHAPTER TWENTY

The funeral and Madame Baker's slip

F UNERALS ARE SAD. A double funeral is even more sorrowful—especially the one for Mose Baker, whose body was never found, and Fish. Mose Baker had never said a word to me while we were in the boat together searching for Fish, so as I thought about the last time I had spoken to them, Friday leaving the pool room, I felt a twinge of guilt, especially remembering my suspicions. When we attended the ceremony on Sunday, I was still exhausted and bruised from the fight I'd had to put up in the water, and I'd caught a real bad cold. Every time I sneezed, my mother and my father gave me a concerned look. They understood, but Reverend Black looked down at me from his pulpit sharply. He should have known I wasn't coughing for my pleasure.

Looking around, I saw nearly as many white faces as black. Our church was suddenly integrated. I guess I'll never understand white people. Without Old Rufus' boats, and the help of some other white men, Fish's body would've never been recovered. If it hadn't been for Skip Goodweather, I would've joined Mose Baker over the falls and probably never been found either. Still, Skip Goodweather, just to name one, had been the nastiest of all to Fish. Now Skip and Betsy were sitting just a few pews away from my family and me.

Mr. Pete and every last one of his cronies were noticeably absent. That said a lot.

Some came today out of curiosity—to see the hole in Fish's chest. They got cheated: Fish's casket stayed closed. I saw just as many falsely solemn-looking black people who I knew had been nasty to Fish, too. All of Duck Tanner's bunch were present, with sad faces, including Short Billy, who had good reason. Some faces were sad because now they'd have to do their own work. I coughed again and drew another hard look from Reverend Black. He had been chosen to officiate, but since he'd always used Fish to mow his lawn for free, he had nothing to look so saintly for.

Toad Man sat near us, but on the end near my dad and farthest away from Grandma, because she couldn't stand to be close to him. He had the most innocent of looks, and he was clean, for once, and even smelled somewhat good. I saw why. His secret love, the widow Mrs. Baby Doll Long, never missed funerals. She had come all painted and perfumed up, and

247

not in black, like most folks. Showing his usual lack of respect, too, Toad Man was gaping over in her direction instead of up front.

Big Shack was still locked up in jail. Tommy had already been sent off to reform school in a hurry for his own safety, because a few white people in town had been saying it would be best to hang him. It was probably just talk, and nothing more, but those sensitive words brought back awful memories. A few members of the black community (my father among them) went and had a talk with the sheriff. For once Zeke didn't take any chances.

Tommy's was sure one name Bird would never mention in our house again. Mad Doc Holden was the only other person who hadn't shown up in church. He was so out of touch, most likely he didn't know.

I was feeling a little out of touch too. I was finding it real hard to figure all the people out—my own dad, for instance, who'd kept some secrets from me that I'd had to find out from Mose Baker. However, Mose was right: My dad probably did it to keep from scaring me, because now that I knew, I didn't feel the same about the world anymore. And although Mose Baker had been more than a puzzle himself, I somehow had felt I could trust him. There were a lot more questions I had never asked him. One minute he was there, looking at me as the boat began to rip apart—then he wasn't. It showed me just how dangerous it was to get too close to people.

And I still couldn't understand how Mr. Pete and

the others could get away with what they did. Nobody had done a thing then, back when it happened. Still nothing has been done. Nobody has ever even brought the subject up, once. I couldn't walk around for the rest of my life with this inside, pretending that nothing had happened. The thought gave me a chill.

"Now, let us bow our heads for a moment of silent prayer for Sergeant Mose Baker, the beloved brother whose heroic efforts were in vain . . ." I heard Reverend Black say, and clear his throat. It was the end of the ceremony, the very last thing before we were to file out behind Fish's casket.

I had missed most of it, thinking about Mose Baker's body, alone, cold, floating along the river, somewhere between Sun City and the Gulf of Mexico, probably.

At the edge of the cemetery, after Fish's burial, Madame Baker whispered to me through her veil, asking if I would join her at home for a quiet moment.

The house was full of overly sweet flowers. Pictures of Fish and Mose Baker haunted every room. There was enough food lying around to feed an army. No other visitors stayed any longer than it took to drop off a basket of food and whisper a quick condolence. It was probably guilt.

Neither of us had much appetite. We just sat around the kitchen table together quietly, where Fish, Mose, and I had nibbled on the madame's nauseating hamburgers a few days before. Again the madame hadn't cleared away her beauty-parlor accessories yet, so we sat amid a sea of bottles. The gifts of food were wedged into the vacant spaces; the floor was still littered with cut hair. The beauty-parlor odors mixed with the food scents.

Besides all kinds of fruit, most of the gifts of food were stuff you could eat cold or heat up again like fried chicken, baked chicken, and turkey. The steaks and link sausages had to be eaten right away—if not, they'd go bad. Though the spinach and the collard greens hadn't spoiled yet, because of the intense heat their flavor was already getting strong. They'd have to be eaten in a hurry too. Madame Baker gave me a big steak, a long link of sausage, a large portion of rice, and more spoons of string beans than I could eat. She took the same, but less. Cokes were lying on the kitchen counter, hot. Madame Baker apologized for forgetting to put water in the fridge to cool. I said I wasn't thirsty.

I wasn't hungry either. I picked at my plate, like the madame did, not really eating, just going through the motions, thinking. Madame Baker had had her husband dragged from his bed in the middle of the night and lynched. She had just lost two sons to the river. She was all alone now. What was she going to do? Finally, I got up and left the table. I wandered over to the back screen door, which looks out over the river. I got interested in Mose Baker's summer garden to keep my mind off other things.

Madame Baker startled me when she spoke suddenly. "Thanks for what you did for Fish."

250

I looked away from the garden, wondering if she was aware I had been staring at it. I cut around to face her, but I couldn't see her eyes clearly behind her dark veil. Still I felt her stare boring into me. "I didn't really do anything."

"Now that's not true at all, Bones, and you know it. You've done an awful lot, and I want to thank you," she said.

Perhaps, I thought, she hadn't noticed the direction of my stare. So I didn't see any fault in asking, "Just what in the world do you have planted out there in that bald spot in your garden?"

I saw her begin to tremble, and it was not because of any grief.

"Just some seeds I planted—late." The bitterness in her voice shocked me. It was the same quick answer Mose had given me that last day in the pool room.

Mose Baker had tended the little garden. Madame Baker was lying, but her tears were genuine.

"I'd better be going," I said.

We were in the kitchen. The back door was the quickest way out. The river trail was just off her garden, and also the shortest cut to my boat, which was still moored out front of the barbershop, where I had left it on Friday. Still, Madame Baker walked me all the way down her long dark hallway to the front door, and I could feel her watching me, every step of the way.

"Good-bye, Bones," she said from behind the musty door just before pushing it into the lock with a loud click.

Thinking of her, how she had acted, how she had looked, the little I had seen of her behind her dark veil, I wandered even farther off my way and bumped into Skip Goodweather standing on the sidewalk outside the Bar & Grill. In the late-afternoon sun our long shadows overlapped.

It had been his quick thinking that had recovered Fish's corpse from the rapids and saved my life. When I realized he was staring at me, I changed my expression and tried to think of something to say. Considering what was on my mind, I must've had a real strange look on my face, though it couldn't have been half as strange as what Skip shocked me by doing.

"Looks like you could use a cold Coke," Skip said, and he actually reached his hand up and patted my shoulder, sort of.

I was speechless.

"And it's on the house," Skip added.

I was thirsty, but there was something more important on my mind. Still, I felt I had to say, "Reckon it's me who owes you one, and maybe—tomorrow—I just might drop by and take you up on that Coke." I took a breath. "Though don't let that make you think I'm going to let you off so easy at the next rodeo. You didn't beat me but by not even a whole inch."

"My trophy's six inches taller than yours, though," Skip said through a cautious smile that told me he knew the way I felt about Mose Baker and Fish.

"And it'll be mine next year," I boasted back, urging a smile.

"You wanna bet, Bonapart?" Skip said. Then a big bear's "Ho-ho-ho!" erupted from his puffed-up chest. Inside that thick head, maybe Skip Goodweather's changed some. I thought, I sure hope he never ever turns out to be the way his father was.

The sound of Skip's laughter was still ringing in my ears when I reached the landing and eased down into my boat.

CHAPTER TWENTY-ONE

The summer garden

I DIDN'T GO STRAIGHT HOME. Much later, taking my time, I rowed slowly upriver and faded into the nightfall. When it was dark enough, I doubled back downriver and drifted slowly toward Madame Baker's. My heart thumped steadily louder the closer I got.

I banked behind the Jeffersons', the backyard before the madame's. There was no mud bar. I threw my rock anchor up the bank, forgetting the loud thud it would make when it fell. I tied the bow string to a bush that scratched my hand. Cautiously, I climbed up the bank to take the river trail the rest of the way.

The Jeffersons were eating a late dinner. I heard Mabel's brothers arguing over who would get the last pork chop. I double-checked every few feet and stepped lightly as I crept. There was nobody on the

254

river trail except me.

As I inched toward Madame Baker's backyard and got closer to her garden, my feet got heavier every step I took. Butterflies fluttered around in the pit of my stomach and crawled up my throat. I tried to convince myself it was just hunger pains. My nervousness also broke me out in a cold sweat. But I soon saw I had no reason to be nervous. The house was dark; Madame Baker was gone—I saw just what I was afraid I'd see, and my heart skipped a beat!

Where Mose Baker's garden had been, a neat little mound of dirt had been freshly turned.

Would Madame Baker leave town with the money?—I had hoped she would give it back, or put it in a place where some honest person would find it. Would she leave before Mose's body was found? (Or did Mose Baker somehow survive the falls again?) If I had lost all my family—the way she did—what would I do?

I didn't hang around too long. Before anybody saw me, I went back down the bank and got into my boat, and let the current carry me lazily downriver a ways before I got up the energy to row.

Down near where Shack's bridge once stood I stopped. I thought about Fish, and Mose, and the old oak tree in the swamp, and I thought about Skip saving my life. Finally I leaned into the oars to head back upriver into Abernathy's Swamp.

An Afterword

In January, this year, in 1992, I saw a cross burning. It made me think about Mr. Pete and his friends, which made me think about Mose Baker, something I hadn't done for a very long time.

About the Author

Ray Prather was born in Florida and was educated at the Cooper Union in New York City. He has lived in Europe and Africa, traveled extensively in Asia, and has written and illustrated books that have been published in the United States, Kenya, and Tanzania. Mr. Prather has worked free-lance for the European television and film industries. He calls Florida home.

This is his first book for HarperCollins.